ZERO
VISIBILITY
POSSIBLE

ZERO VISIBILITY POSSIBLE

A Novel by

NINA BURLEIGH

FOUR STICKS PRESS

"*How many of us are really wounded by the stories
we tell? How many of us really invest our deepest selves
in the reality of the world, whether it's painful or not?
I wonder about that.*"
   –Charles Pierce

"*At the center of this story, there is a terrible secret,
a kernel of cyanide, and the secret is that the story doesn't
matter, doesn't make any difference, doesn't figure.*"
   –Joan Didion

This is a work of fiction. Names, characters, businesses,
places, events, locales, and incidents are either the products
of the author's imagination or used in a fictitious manner.
Any resemblance to actual persons, living or dead,
or actual events is purely coincidental.

The author is grateful to the following people and institutions
for their support: Barbara Bourland, Jorge Colombo,
Larry Doyle, Greg Olear, Valerie Plame, Peter Riva,
Joe Shepherd, Western New Mexico University, and
the Metochi Study Center Writing Retreat.

Cover and book design: Jorge Colombo

ISBN: 979-8-89079-304-1 (paperback)
ISBN: 979-8-89079-305-8 (ebook)

1. THE MAN IN THE WINDOW

Las Vegas, 11:11 p.m. Monday

Under American skies, where eagles soar high,
I thank God for this land so free-eee-ee.
From amber waves of grain to mountains majesty,
Lord's liberty shines on me.

Twenty-two thousand people are in the audience, and at least half are singing along with Jonny K Blue on the Vegas strip at the True Grit Country music festival. Voices carry. Closer to the ground are ripples of laughter and hoo-hahs, sloshing plastic cups, and sticky bodies jostling. Tattooed white skin in tiny tank tops with golden Eagle heads. Cowboy hats, cowboy boots. MAGA hats. Flags. American flag towels around shoulders, flag doo-rags. Some people brought kids. They wave flags on tiny sticks.

Blue and the band are engulfed in stage smoke. A pair of red, white, and blue towers of light rise from the haze and pierce the void of desert sky. The Twin Towers of Old Glory. Music rises with the light towers; sound and glow dissipate somewhere in the stratosphere. American spirits time traveling on a light bridge into the Milky Way.

The True Grit is an *outdoor* music event in name only. This stretch of the Strip is as indoor as it is possible to be and still be outside. Neon and glass. The air smells air-conditioned or canned, like the oxygen coursing through ICU ventilators or maybe the International Space Station.

> *With a hand on my heart and a prayer on my lips,*
> *I salute our flag, and the freedom it grips,*
> *And the soldiers who fought, and those who still fight.*
> *Their sacrifice echoes through days and nights.*
> *In this land of the brave, freedom ain't free*
> *Lord's liberty shines on me…*

The air vibrates with thousands of voices. There are many patriots here. Not a few have hands on their hearts. A few wipe at tears.

Blue was on his second "Lords's liberty shines" when the shooting started.

Pop! Pop! Pop! Pop! Pocketypop! Pop!

Sounded like firecrackers at first to everyone—except the gun enthusiasts, of whom, at this event, there were not a few. They knew the sound of automatic weapons fire when they heard it before the bodies started to fall.

For the first thirty seconds, the band played on. Blue stopped singing just before security rushed onstage. A screech from colossal speakers followed the last guitar chord. By then, horror was rippling out from the middle of the crowd. The first bodies were down. The inhuman *Pop! Pop! Pop! Pppoppopopopopopopopop!* continued, a staccato metronome to the screams.

No one was listening by then. One thought only: *Where is the EXIT?* But what is an exit under a sky raining bullets? They need interiors, ceilings, doors, walls, and tunnels.

Half the crowd surged toward a five-foot-high chain link fence. Those who could hoisted themselves over it. More were crushed against it. The fence made them better individual targets because, oh, yes, he had a scope. For a second, bodies fell off the wall; then, the shooter aimed his spray back into the disintegrating pack in the middle of the street.

For ten minutes, the man on the 32nd floor of the Mandalay Bay gazed down on the faux daylight of the Vegas night and fired no less than 3,000 bullets. He had chosen the Vista Suite for this view, and when the reservations desk made an error and tried to put him in a different one, he threw a fit, an outburst recorded by the lobby camera and later viewed hundreds of times by police.

It would later be said that Bill Meadows was living out a long-cherished fantasy of shooting human fish in a barrel. He'd once earned five million dollars from a single video poker game in the same building where he took his firing position. A high roller and brilliant gamer, he beat the system.

This was video poker of another sort.

It had taken him two days and five trips up and down the

elevators with a luggage trolley to bring all the necessary equipment up. Some of his guns could hit their targets at five hundred yards. He'd bought them all at gun shows in Arizona, Nevada, and Texas—legally.

Stockpiled. Cached by the dozen. You never knew when the government would try to stop the trade.

Oh, and ammo. Thousands of rounds.

The sellers would not remember him.

There were records, of course. No man eludes them entirely. But his name was so common and his face so average. He was Everyman. He was no one. He had lived in multiple states. He had twenty-five addresses in the previous dozen years.

Conspiracy speculators hit Reddit minutes after his name was published. They swarmed a new thread under r/conspiracy — R/vegas and speculated.

Anything could be said of a man after a scene like this.

Shooter was a military-industrial complex *ghost*.

ISIS, White ISIS.

He was laundering drug money. He was putting dirty dollars into the Wynn properties and taking clean dollars out.

Gamblers or people claiming to be posted on the thread. Over the last ten years, one or two had spotted Bill Meadows in high-roller VIP rooms. He was colorless, glassy-eyed, and easily forgotten. Diffident. On Valium. Often flanked by bored-looking sylphic young women.

He didn't have much to say.

Was he even just one man?

Time should have provided some answers.

But none came, only unreliable witnesses, shrouded employment history, and half-answers to every question. Facts, suppositions, and lies floated around the black hole of him, and *pfft!* he was reduced, an infinitesimal element in impenetrable mass.

Up high, at the edges of the smashed Vista window, the desert breeze blew the drapes in and out, raspy whisper, like the sound of last breaths. The sound of real human terror and agony was distant and dreamy, muffled by the toilet paper he'd stuffed in his ears. He would not completely noise-cancel this event with his gun-range headphones.

Oh, no.

This was the chorus of angels that would carry him into his eternal rest as he placed one of the pistols in his mouth and pulled the trigger.

2. THE ONES AND THE ZEROS

New York, 1:11 a.m. Tuesday

"Fuck off. Do you really think you'd be here if you hadn't married a Pulitzer?"

Marjorie DuBois wakes from a shallow sleep. The moment of waking coincides with a wave of prickling skin. Full body panic. Her mind is a small rodent, skittering away from the light of consciousness toward the dark edges after having scratched up, in a split second, unpaid debt, a bad boyfriend, a declining career, expanding thighs, and advancing age. Ultimately death.

All that, plus a fit of *esprit d'escalier,* which wasn't exactly what the insomniac brain rat was pawing after, just the nearest irritant.

Petty stuff, a rat-snack.

Marjorie had been at a gathering mere hours ago. The dinner party was at one of the 5th Avenue multi-floor apartments inhabited by a couple whose ancestors included Americans in the War of 1812, present at the founding of the UN and Jackie Kennedy's White House parties. On this night, around the vast table were the hosts, plus the ambassador of Finland and his wife, a pair of hoary Nobel prize winners (chemistry, economics) and their wives, and the chair of Yale Jackson School of Global Affairs. And the dinner honorees: two nearly mute alabaster men, Swedish business executives from the Nobel Prize committee.

Marjorie Dubois, invited by the ambassador, was seated between two of the mutes. She was the kind of single woman-about-town that *salonistes* and consulates kept on their lists to bring some, but not too much, heat to their events. Marjorie had played her part, cashing out a few tidbits of gossip about the President's Adderall habit and his latest Oval Office meltdown. Europeans, like the dinner honorees, were avid to know more about Nazis in the White House.

She smiled politely as a physics laureate in his eighties sang "Chances Are" *acapella* while everyone nodded and applauded. It was excruciating. Obsequiousness had its applications at border crossings and police stations. But gratuitous unctuousness, even if for deserving and ancient icons, made her restless. If only the hosts had invited a French playboy, a randy Fiat heir, or any man with a look in his eye.

She regretted coming even before the incident.

Right before dinner, she slipped away from the group through the galley kitchen where the staff was at work. She was headed to the bathroom more to regroup than to pee. She needed a moment to gut-check herself in a mirror.

She was stopped en route by Poppy Thurgood.

Poppy was an artist-slash-photographer, ambitious, married to an award-winning war correspondent turned Yale department chair. Tiny, dark, and pretty, she had not quite accidentally become her then-married boyfriend's baby mama while in Iraq. Marjorie didn't know her well, but she knew something about Poppy, something many journalists who had worked in Iraq knew. A war zone rookie, trying to "connect with" and charm an old Shia cleric whose portrait she was shooting with a Hasselblad, she'd dropped the name of one of the press pack's favorite Iraqi fixers. She said she was so grateful to Ahmed, who had led her into that "lovely, lovely little shrine" in Najaf and into the "stunning" *mihrab*. The old cleric took very seriously rules about women in the holy places. Poppy had indirectly got Ahmed killed.

Now, Poppy had a nameplate of her own on a door at Yale School of Art, and she had a toddler and was the wife to the toddler's father. The thinking went that Ahmed would have died anyway.

"Marjorie! *What* are you doing here?"

Smiling, sharp as a Japanese knife.

"Ambassador K invited me," she replied. "And you?"

Poppy's expression morphed into an unsettling fusion of embarrassment and triumph.

"He didn't tell the Ashforths," she whispered, "about inviting you. I think Mrs. A had to get the staff to rustle up another chair and setting for you at the table. And now, her seating is off—odd number. She's a little upset. She was chewing out the social secretary in the kitchen."

Marjorie took in the bold stare. The moment demanded a tart retort or humiliation. At that instant, Marjorie was repressing the earworm "Everybody plays the fool, sometimes—no exception to the rule" that had installed itself in her head since last weekend when Lochinvar—as she called her lover in her mind, *Oh, Lochinvar!*—had sent his crushing email about meeting "someone perfect for me" while at a conference in Spain. Replete with details, the message sent her to a tile floor in a DC hotel bathroom in the fetal position.

She looked at Poppy, feeling like she was waking up from a trance. It was a measure of her collapse that she was mute. And that the proper reply would only occur to her hours later, useless, alone in her bed.

"But don't worry, it's okay! We calmed her down." And off she went.

Of course, Poppy loathed her. Many women did.

Marjorie DuBois, award-winning investigative journalist and bringer-down of senators and generals, had long legs and rambunctious breasts that were difficult to confine, even had she wanted to. She was often photographed by *British Vogue* and other publications in designer clothes in Baghdad and other war-torn countries. Amal Clooney calls her a friend. A "sexy Bob Woodward," as one of the many magazine features on her had put it. She saves refugees, loves sex, and has had too many lovers to count. She gave a married UN officer hickeys in Africa just before he had to fly home to his wife in Oslo. She also ran off to Greece with another reporter's husband for a month and seduced the occasional UN ambassador or Senate staffer for a lead.

She was unrepentant—put the B in bold.

Still very much in play.

Now, in the dark, very much on the plummet down a long slide, the untouchable Ms. DuBois was obsessively, secretly in love with a retrograde man who was tending his personal pussy farm on Tinder and Bumble. He claimed to be hunting for a wife to give him daily intimacy, plus cook and mother some children. Whore in the bedroom, servant in the house.

And *that* she—Marjorie Dubois—would never be. Still, she was smitten, sick with it.

> *O, young Lochinvar is come out of the west.*
> *Through all the wide border, his steed was the best,*
> *And save his good broadsword, he weapons had none;*
> *He rode all unarmed, and he rode all alone.*
> *So faithful in love and so dauntless in war,*
> *There never was a knight like the young Lochinvar.*

Steve Burns—her Lochinvar—was beautiful. And he came out of the West, a cyber security geek by day, weaving ones and zeroes into the digital mesh that mesmerized, tracked, and tormented the world. By night, transformed, he was solitary and unarmed except for his broadsword, an accouterment that she, there was no other word for it, worshipped. He probably would soon dance a bride out the door, like Sir Walter Scott's fair knight.

Stalking (due diligence) easily turned up that the latest

"perfect for me" in Spain had an advanced degree in physics and taught Pilates. So, she could do backbends on him in bed while discussing black holes. Marjorie marveled at the copious abundance and wide variety in the pool of available women online—not for the first time.

She'd never had a problem with competition. Men were like buses; another one always came along. A legendary voluptuous creature but now with thighs, she saw it if no one else did yet, running toward zaftig. Sophia Loren's lips were beginning to sag. She saw that too, even if no one else did.

Besides the romantic crisis, something else was splintering her. The pace of events in the world and her life had started to resemble the whirring calendar in an old movie. Days spun into months into years. Moving at speed with events had tuned her to a higher frequency and then, apparently, zapped her.

The prickling sleeplessness started in late 2014, after Sinjar. As had been her practice for twenty years, she boarded the first plane to get as close as possible to the outbreak of war. This time, she landed at a camp a few dozen miles from where ISIS had massacred men and kidnapped Yezidi women and girls. Marjorie interviewed raped mothers who had watched their daughters being raped. She talked to young women impregnated by gang rapists. Some of them were strangely calm and matter of fact. Some were deranged. Many were simply catatonic.

She stayed for three months, mostly talking to women, children, and old folks. Almost no males between the ages of twelve and sixty-five. They drifted into the camp, glassy-eyed, gray-cheeked, lips dry, sick in body and soul. The women told harrowing stories of how the women they didn't murder right away were being traded around in an industrial scale sex trafficking operation.

And no one in the world could do anything about it.

Back in New York after that, she understood that something *had* happened to her. At night, only shallow sleep and colorless dreams. She had their snapshots in her head: the woman sitting in the dark; the braids of the French aid worker explaining how that one, over there, couldn't speak, was mute from trauma; a child without an eye; and an old man weeping in a wheelchair.

The Yezidi survivors of ISIS were in black and white. So were the mothers waiting in line outside Baghdad hospital, cuddling malnourished babies, wrinkled little faces like carved shrunken apples. There was so much trauma and grief—an avalanche of it. She had not forgotten them but drained them of color and heat. An automatic button inside just converted them.

All in black and white.

Most days, she could forget about the eerie, emotionless world her sleeping brain conjured. When the sun rose, the end-of-the-world sensation slept like a vampire. Night was another thing. Jolting awake, she couldn't tell what came first: panic activating adrenal glands or vice versa.

She could run a footrace right now. There is no going back to sleep, not for a while. Maybe, she thinks as she gropes for the phone on the table in the dark beside her pillow, she has managed to sleep until almost dawn.

But no, it is on the screen: 1:11 a.m., less than two hours

since she lay her head on the pillow.

The trio of ones had its usual effect. She thought of Lacey, the divorced mother in Menlo Park with her suburban blonde bob, freckled, bare arms, and magenta dress. A California sunset. Sipping Oregon pinot on the deck of a sleek, woody Silicon Valley bistro bar.

Lacey's grief joined a stream Marjorie had coaxed out, transcribed, cut for space, and published. Between wars, an editor had dispatched her to investigate a rash of suicides related to smartphone-recorded sexual assaults. At the time, it was new. This one was only different because it happened at a party with the sons of tech titans. They recorded themselves assaulting a nude, rag-doll body. Blacked out from Vodka, Cheyenne didn't remember any of it. The video went viral in her high school, and the fifteen-year-old was dead a week later. Lacey had heard the hum of the car motor when she came home from work, and knew, before she even opened the garage door.

Five years on, Marjorie remembered a mother's talisman. In the days after her daughter died, Lacey saw ones whenever she looked at her phone, alarm clock, or even the time and temperature display at the Wells Fargo billboard in downtown San Jose. It was always 1:11 or 11:11. And you know what? Never on purpose.

Early in her grief, a psychic friend told her that seeing time in that pattern meant angel beings were nearby. The ones were a form of digital messaging, a *thin place*, a space-time quantum chink in the wall between this world and the next.

"I know it sounds weird," Lacey said. "But I can feel Cheyenne at those times. I can feel her right there on the other side," her voice broke.

Marjorie secretly hoped that the little superstition was true for Lacey's sake and even maybe for her own. She'd inadvertently adopted it herself; a little awareness popped up whenever she saw ones, like not stepping on a crack or you'll break your mother's back. If you paid attention and never stepped on a crack, your mother's back stayed intact. Marjorie had never really believed that but skipped over the cracks anyway.

The digits on the screen had advanced futureward: 1:12, another minute of potential sleep wasted in full consciousness.

Marjorie pulled the phone off the bedside table and opened it. Typed a query into Google.

What is the meaning of 11:11?

A page of links glowed blue in the dark.

"11:11 is the number of masters. The ascended masters are sending you the message that you are a divine aspect of the Universe, a master at being yourself."

Marjorie snorted. It was all bullshit. Enough.

She put the phone back on the table in the dark and lay back on the pillow, willing her brain to go under. At the edge of consciousness, the phone bleeped, not the Apocalyptic wail of bad weather warnings and lost child alerts that simultaneously lit up everyone's phones in New York City. A news event. She ignored it, but it bleeped again and then again and again. Updates in quick succession. A major happening, something dire.

Earthquake. Tsunami. War.

The beeping wouldn't stop. Marjorie rolled over in the dark, groaned, thumbed the phone, and clicked through the glowing headlines: "Mass Shooting in Las Vegas. Hundreds wounded. Death toll uncertain. Extremely high casualties. Historic." There was a video of screaming panic, and the popcorn pop of shots in the dark was already inside her phone, in her ears and eyeballs. Hers and a billion others.

A clench of despair seized her stomach, before, by habit, she willed it away with conscious and increasingly, she suspected, perverse, professional curiosity. The shield was cracked but still functional:

Who? What? Why?

Well, there it was, tomorrow's news, tonight.

3. #VEGASMASSACRE IS DOING REALLY WELL

Lower Manhattan, 9:00 a.m. Tuesday

"I'll do guns," Brickett said.

Vera Rogers, Rutgers '07 and managing editor, leads another morning meeting of newsmaggots at *NewsMag* HQ. It's an under-attended meeting, as usual. Most of the staff is not physically present. They are wherever they sit with the laptops tapping—their beds, Starbucks, a barstool—churning out early morning stories to meet the company's click demand and earn the daily salary add-on that just covered rent on the dirty-sock and cumin-scented Bed Stuy quadruple share.

Okay, not the journalism she'd learned in school, but you take what you can get, right?

Vera wanted to be a journalist since she was a kid growing up in Teaneck, one of the Jersey-bedroom communities she could almost see now from the office windows looking west across the Hudson River. She was a ten-year-old in 1991, prone on her belly and in love with Christiane Amanpour and the Scud Stud on TV in the Gulf War. Now a sleeve-tattooed genius of an editor, Vera has been managing editor since her former boss, the executive editor, was sacked. Too old, too male, too white, and not on board with the new regime. It happened.

Vera is smart both ways. Equanimity is her middle name. High "EQ" on the intake test and good management material. Unruffled even when her old boss announced at a company-wide staff meeting, in his way of praise, that she was "a love-muffin I just want to hug." She didn't run to HR. She knew he meant well.

She has put out the fires, overseen hires and sacks, run an eye over the stream of copy, and fixed what she could for the last year. The owners of the shell of a legacy media brand never meddled with her domain. Asteroid impacts, aliens, and great investigative work were all the same—all about the eyeballs.

It's the future of journalism; she gets it. Every day, she gives the staff a pep talk, the staff that bothers to show up in the office before noon. Most are unwilling to give up screen time that could be spent dashing off news about Alzheimer's cures or the supervolcano that will bury the entire American continent in thirty feet of ash.

The President has declared what they do "fake news."

Indeed, it might be!

At first, it was a joke. Before long, it dawned on some of them that no matter how much they fact-checked, a significant segment of the population believed they were just making it up. So, why not stop checking?

And really, one could be making it up: People believed what they wanted to believe now. Wounded school shooting survivors were crisis actors. Hillary drank the blood of babies. The US government was preparing to throw Christians in FEMA camps.

The clock was running out on agreed-upon reality, but Vera clung to the rules like a sailor lashed to the mast in a storm. For the moment, it was all triage. She encouraged the kids working for minimum wage, producing aggregated clickbait to come up with independent ideas. The experienced elders were more of a challenge. Most were falling apart at the seams, overwhelmed by the cascade of insane events, the loosening of all rigor. In another time, in another company, *the way it used to be*, they would each have taken months to report just one of the stories of the day—and been nominated for a Pulitzer.

Each day, she gives a talk, some version of this: "These are crazy times. We can't all do our jobs the way we always have. I know that. But we want you to keep doing work you can be proud of! We have to do that work. Build a really good team. Own the beat. Bring excitement to your area of expertise."

On this day, five staff members are assembled. They stare at their phones and wait to be called upon to account for their beats. There's a speakerphone in the middle of the table for those not present in person. Every once in a while, the speaker emits a cough, fart, bark, doorbell, or cat's meow.

"Mute, please!"

"What the fuck is happening in Vegas?"

She surveys the assemblage. There's Brickett, a hot young police and crime reporter. Today belongs to him. He knows it, giddy. Vera knew his limitations, but Brickett truly cared about his click count, not just the daily bonus. So what if he was a little slow? Enthusiasm was in short supply around here, and he had it.

He had been up since early morning, slamming out #vegasmassacre updates in separate files with different headlines. The off-track betting-style gray TV screens placed strategically around the room, with headlines jostling against each other, rising and falling as the tracker crawled the clicks, advertised his triumph.

All three of Brickett's short takes are at the top.

"Ten minutes."

"Twelve gunfire bursts. Sixty-five killed. More than five hundred injured."

"High roller shooter gambled after dark and slept during the day, disliked being in the sun."

Vera happened to know that one of the gnomes on the editorial desk, a foot out the door of the profession hoping to hold on until Medicare kicked in, had plugged the word "vampire" into that last headline earlier.

Vera caught it before it went live.

"So, #VegasMassacre is doing really well. Let's continue to tap into the trend. Open to ideas for some takes for the rest of the morning. Brickett can't do them all."

Vera paused, looked up, and made eye contact with the two interns and the "health and wellness" reporter, who was sucking on a straw submerged in a toad green smoothie.

"Opportunities for the rest of you. Enterprise," she said.

She looked at the interns, two college kids from somewhere in the South, maybe Alabama or Tennessee. They looked like pink lambs.

"Social media, we need you to keep sweeping the sites for fresh video. Fresh real-time views are still being posted. Scrape them and upload updates to our story."

"Guns—where did he buy them? His addiction was video poker; can we get a health and wellness take on how gambling addictions work and affect mental health? I'm seeing the "Who is Bill Meadows" pieces all over now, but I think there's more, and we haven't done a comprehensive one. Can we do some aggregated pickup?"

Brickett was palming his phone. He got up to leave. "I need to take some calls."

Now, there were three in the room, plus an unknown number of ghosts in the machine. Vera could never be sure who all was on the conference call—any number of staff in their Brooklyn apartments and the two men in DC.

She had learned to ID some by the sounds of their cats, others by their coughs.

"Washington? You on? Let's get the White House response

written up," she said. "Preston, you there?" Silence. "And Chris, have we tried the FBI or ATF?"

Preston Silver, senior national affairs writer, could hear Vera, but he wasn't going to deign to speak to her. His cat could speak for him. Princeton, magna cum laude. The American history '88 author of the critically acclaimed one-hit wonder on the '92 election and its less-read follow-up on the '96 election was, at that moment, in his underwear in his kitchen in DuPont Circle, microwaving takeout Chinese from the night before.

He thought he might put in the call she wanted when he was finished eating and scrolling his Tinder feed. He had more pressing business: seeking a replacement for his ex-wife, the Silicon Valley communications guru and now Senator Carla Silver from the great state of Maine, who was threatening to cut off alimony.

A few miles away, in a townhouse in Arlington, Christopher H. Goodman, a national security writer, was also listening in and grunted assent. Chipper clickbait apologist Vera annoyed the hell out of him. Heart in the right place. *So goddamn green.* It didn't seem likely that she and "the team" could get a toehold into this story. All the big guns were hours ahead on it.

The New York Times reported that the gunman had been a legit businessman who made a lot of money on smart real estate investments. He managed buildings in California and New Mexico. He was an employee of the US government before that. Maybe at the Post office or the IRS? Or an accountant at the Department of Defense? A faceless bureaucrat.

He owned a Cessna and flew it.

Recently, he took lots of luxury cruises.

He had been a college math whiz.

His success only "deepened the mystery," reporters were writing.

Goodman was a Gulf War vet, Army intelligence, with good CIA and FBI contacts—a few too many of them grizzled and fighting off cancers or undiagnosable debilitating post-war maladies like his.

Dying daily, or if alive, fading out of the loop.

Still, he had a network.

He was scrolling that list of contacts, trying to decide which of his sources would be most willing to explain why a Bill Meadows—who looked an awful lot like the Bill Meadows alleged Vegas shooter in the *Washington Post* that morning— was also in a group photo taken in Central America of a bunch of CIA bush pilots from 1981. Captioned by name.

That morning, a source had emailed Goodman a scan of the photograph in black and white. He stared at the grainy image from a retired agents' newsletter: Honduras, palm trees, landing strip, jungle, seven men.

Meadows' face was indistinct. But still, there he seemed to be, captioned with his name, among a dozen others. Now, could anyone say with certainty that this Meadows was the same guy as the glassy-eyed balding white guy in the broken window with the guns?

How many sixty-something Bill Meadows would there be with pilots' licenses?

Quite a few, probably.

That was the nature of the gray man, the spook, the American *sicario*. There he would be, among a thousand Bill Meadows, blending in with the suburban car dealers, insurance salesmen, real estate agents, stockbrokers, and high school math teachers.

However, the name and face were in the CIA's former agent newsletter. What the fuck was that particular Bill Meadows doing at CIA in 1981?

By no chance was Goodman about to announce this gem to Vera and whichever kids were in the meeting room in New York. This was his IP, and only his, for now. He clicked out of the video call without saying a word and called up a webpage of direct flights to Vegas.

He didn't take pleasure in dissing the young woman. Well, maybe a little bit. Okay, he was a fat-phobic asshole at heart. He could not respect a young woman with sleeve tattoos hired for her expertise in digital media. It wasn't her. It was what she represented. He fired up his fifth Merit of the morning.

Fuck it all.

And yet, if he put the pedal to the metal of his rattly 2007 Jeep Cherokee, he might be able to make the noon nonstop Reagan National to McCarran. He threw his laptop, clean shirt, and toothbrush into a duffel and walked outside. It was dry and bright and smelled of verdant Washington, DC, in autumn. His neighbors' roses were still blooming.

4. TRUE LOVE AND THERAPY

New York, 10:00 a.m. Tuesday

Five hundred miles north in Manhattan, lines of double-parked trucks hissed along the curb. Horns blared; cyclists swerved. The stream of humanity stopped, started, and stopped again at the cross-street lights on the avenues. Like a flock of birds or ants, moving as one, keyed to some invisible biological vibration.

Marjorie Dubois was inside this thick surge, a little raw after an appointment with a therapist. A therapist. It was still hard to believe she had joined that club.

She had noticed a habit lately of deep sleep just before dawn. That's when she had her dreams. This morning, she woke up with a single flicker of a scene in mind: A dog was running along the rocks by a river. She was watching, followed by a man, walking too close to the rocks, looking for something. It was the Hudson River, near the bike path, under the Trump condos, where the owners had voted to tear off the name. Sunsets were gorgeous over New Jersey's back down there. It wasn't a bad dream, but its uneasy residue clung to her.

She remembered the dream but didn't remember getting dressed and getting to her appointment—eleven minutes late—at 11:11 a.m., according to her phone.

Amnesia was not a known side effect of the Adderall she sometimes took to concentrate. However, it was a side effect of the Ambien she had gulped down in desperation around 4 a.m.

Was she turning into one of those people, too?

Marjorie had submitted to therapy as an absolute last-ditch desperation measure only after trying a variety of other methods to crush her love obsession: hypnosis; a personal Buddhist chant designed by a monk in Dharamsala; intense exercise; cryotherapy; Monkish, self-imposed loneliness; exotic travel; and long periods of cold-turkey abstinence from all contact with him, including social media stalking.

Nothing had worked to lessen her fascination or break his spell on her. She had lurked and watched as he moved through various women whose Facebook pages were soon transformed into his fan pages. When she'd first discovered this, she'd gotten a fever and was laid up in bed for days, dreaming in erotic technicolor about the various women in his harem.

He was a security-cleared cyber warrior in his late forties—a desk jockey, really, and, she had come to understand, profoundly afraid of the terrorists, the 9/11 Enemy burrowed into his psyche. He lacked her courage and experience abroad. A touch of xenophobic white American suburbia. Yet all he had to do was hit Marjorie with an eggplant emoji, and she was accepting a plane ticket to meet him in Boston or San Francisco or hopping the Acela to DC and a night in the Hay Adams.

A "Mr. Burns" had first approached her by email while she was in Syria. He had offered his services as an anonymous source, feeding her tips about the hunt for ISIS on Protonmail. Eventually, he gave her his name, and she looked him up. He was not terribly discreet for a government cyber spy. He had a Facebook page with pictures of himself surfing. She assumed they were fake. But he was good-looking and his messages sometimes felt seductive. He was, he wrote once, "looking for a journalist to do his bidding."

Months later, back in DC, she met the IRL Mr. Burns at a national security cyber warfare conference.

She searched the faces of the audience at the conference room in the Marriott. He'd spotted her first and sidled up. He wasn't at all what she'd expected. Instead of the basement-dwelling gamer rat who sent her obscure, coder-world tips, she found a California surfer with a crooked smile, blue eyes, and a hank of straight black hair just beginning to be streaked with gray that he kept pushing back off his forehead. He was wearing jeans and hiking boots.

She had managed to speak and then walked outside to sit on a bench and breathe. He had that kind of face.

That was three years ago now.

In the very beginning, it was all fun. She was his Scheherazade, unwinding yarn after yarn from her travels between bouts of sex, basking in the fascination she saw in his eyes. But soon, his attention wandered. And she still had so many stories to tell.

That's when it happened. The floor fell in. What did it all even mean, all those stories, unless filtered through him? There were too many experiences and too many unprocessed impressions.

Three years into what she could only think of as an emotional black hole, she wasn't the sharp girl she had been. It was harder to pay attention. She started making stupid mistakes, one of which brought down a lawsuit that, although settled without fanfare, cost her a coveted contributing writer contract at *The Atlantic*.

The downward slide continued from there. Her mind wandered to him about every thirty seconds—every half minute, like what they say about men and thoughts of sex.

After interviews, whole conversations fell out of her head. When she transcribed them, she heard her voice interjecting the same word repeatedly: *Interesting. Interesting.*

Nothing felt interesting anymore. She only uttered the word as encouragement to keep them talking when she could barely make sense of their words. She could listen later, rewind, listen again, and figure out whether she had reaped anything quotable.

It was bad.

Marjorie couldn't forgive herself for falling into this abyss. And the timing couldn't be worse. Her currency in New

York society was still viable. She was still considered one
of the great brainy beauties. However, at forty-eight, she
was consumed by a wild insecurity. She studied herself in
the mirror with teenage avidity, plucking gray hairs and
examining her face for eyebags and new wrinkles. She found
them every time.

She took the *NewsMag* job because she anticipated needing
better health insurance. A year into her romance with
Lochinvar, she was sick. Her doctor gave her a questionnaire
and assessed her as depressed with high-functioning anxiety.

Desperation drove her to Kara. Kara was close to twenty years
younger and let her sob about the man she called Lochinvar
and about her fear of aging. She had come to this place,
cognitive behavioral therapy offered by NYU, because the
course of treatment promised to be finite. No years of weekly
sessions like some of her friends, working out the same issue
on the same couch for twenty years.

It came with one unusual aspect. The therapy was part of a
research project, and patients had to agree to be videotaped
for future research. Marjorie had assented without much
thought. She'd been so desperately unhappy when she first
entered the tiny office with its two plastic chairs on the ninth
floor above 14th Street. She would have agreed to public
lashing if that promised a cure. And she might have admitted
that she liked the idea of her story recorded and studied, as
she had recorded and listened to hundreds of other people's
stories.

His name was Steve. Almost all the Scrabble letters for
evasive. An MIT brainiac among a Marriott ballroom packed
full of the same—cyber geeks.

Coup de foudre. Love at first sight. She had to walk outside and sit on a bench in the icy January breeze to catch her breath and cool her face before rejoining him for coffee and an in-person interview. Phones were left outside at his request. This wouldn't be recorded. He was cagey as hell right from the start.

She only remembered one other face that, at first sight, provoked such an oxygen-starved time-out. Almost twenty years ago, man-boy, delicious French photographer Guillaume. Lean, draped in cameras, lounging on the clerk's desk in the lobby of the Oloffson Hotel at Port-au-Prince. Potted palms, the *swick-swick* of ceiling fans. Shadows. Strips of sunlight on the floor through the louvered window slats. Heat. Crushing humidity. Everyone was slick with sweat. She was in her late twenties, he ten years younger. He had looked up, and she'd felt dizzy. A greenish swimming pool outside the screen doors was covered with dead palm leaves. Eventually, they stripped and dove in.

The love affair ended when he was blown up three months later while shooting a story on land mines in Sierra Leone. Perhaps if he had lived, he'd have exacted the same toll on her as this man. Maybe they would have lived happily ever after. She would never know.

In the three years since she'd hooked up with her Lochinvar, he had taught her many things about helpless love, new sex tricks, narcissism, jealousy, and maddening lies. She had been an apt pupil. His disappearances were impeccably timed. She couldn't believe they were not calculated to make him more irresistible. For every step he took toward her, he took two backward. His plans were always vague and easily discarded. And there was almost always another woman waiting. He made no secret of it.

In her sessions with Kara, she free-associated, between war stories from years before, when she was whole and courageous, and the story of her now. The delirious joy of the trysts, and more often, the despair of the ghostings, that had occurred between appointments.

"Try to think about what he's replacing, or what you might be doing if you never had met him" Kara said once. Marjorie thought about that for a week, and came back and said she decided that part of his allure had to do with her having lost her grip on how anything else mattered.

"I do remember a time before that when I still believed that what I was doing made a difference in the world." She wiped away tears. But how to identify the point where everything stopped making sense? Maybe with the Yezidi women in Syria? Who could say? Or had it always been just about the adrenalin rush of risk and escaping on a cargo flight out.

She knew she should have hated him. He was a cog in the structure of the machine built on ones and zeroes. The machine had no conception of love, grief, or trauma. It operated according to an inhuman and utterly perfect logic. More often than not, it spewed terrible violence on the world. The ends justified the means.

He had a key into that machine: the security clearance. His preening pride in his access to state security secrets disgusted her. His declarations of patriotism made her cringe. He half-joked about his work: "If I told you about that, I'd have to kill you. Haha…"

Every Wednesday, Kara assigned her homework—like drawing a pie at the end of every day and dividing it into pieces of happiness, anger, sadness, and anxiety. She was supposed to work at making choices to enlarge the happy slice. She was supposed to keep a detailed—hourly, if possible—log of thoughts and the emotions the thoughts instigated.

The rule was: Thought is mother to the emotion. The thought gave birth to the feeling. This could be stopped, still-birthed if caught in time—like a six-week abortion.

She'd been seeing Kara weekly for fourteen weeks and had four to go. She had to admit there was a subtle change in the quality, if not the quantity, of her unhappiness. A bit less dire. A bit more distance. The little exercises helped her identify and amplify little things that made her happy and diminish thoughts that brought her down.

She had admitted many things to Kara beyond love. The dreams, the inability to feel, and seeing grief in black and white. Kara asked whether she thought she funneled all her stifled emotions into her lover. "Maybe," Marjorie said. "Something to consider."

As far as Marjorie was concerned, she had achieved the most important breakthrough by getting to know something important about Ph.D. student therapist Kara.

One day, about ten weeks into their weekly meetings, Marjorie asked Kara what she planned to do with her degree.

"I guess you should know a little more about me," Kara said. Then, after some silence, "I'm an end-of-life therapist," Kara continued.

"End of life?" Marjorie asked. "Geriatric psychology?"

"Yes." As usual, the therapist's gray eyes revealed nothing but professional concern. "Well, yes and no. Most of my patients are in hospice. Not all of them are old."

"Hospice? That's where you work when you're not here?"

"Four afternoons a week," Kara said. "At Mt. Sinai Hospice. It's hard—hard but meaningful."

Marjorie was mortified. She blushed. In a flash of horrifying insight, she saw herself through the eyes of a young woman who counseled dying people, people with the ultimate problem. She sat at their bedsides. What must she make of this privileged, attractive, vibrant woman with a social life and career, wiping snot over incipient middle age and an errant lover?

Of course, Kara would never judge her, all pain being worthy of respect in the praxis. But Marjorie cringed to see her problems through the eyes of a death counselor. The perspective shift was so effective that Marjorie later wondered if Kara's self-reported career path was not part of her therapeutic strategy. In the following weeks, she found she still had much more she wanted to tell Kara. She wanted to entertain her. She liked to make her laugh.

Only occasionally, as she left the building, did she pause to think about the video recording and who might someday watch her tear-stained face. What would they learn? And what a trove that would be for an enemy or—why not?—a future biographer of a very minor early-twenty-first century journalist.

Out on the street, the city was more like Cairo or Delhi every day. Hallucinating men roamed the street in rags, like the naked holy men of the old Muslim cities. Women, limping,

pushing walkers, creeping toward her in wheelchairs, wearing
the paper hospital slippers and wrist tags from a recent night
in the ER. Sidewalks steamed with their smell. Subways were
rolling psych wards.

She nipped into a Starbucks and got in line behind a group
of tourists. American pilgrims in their white tennis shoes
and fanny packs up from Alabama to see the 9/11 Memorial,
Times Square, and the Hard Rock Cafe.

She looked at them, toggling between scorn and impatience
and another feeling, envy. The big city still offered them its
magical aura. As it had to her for the nearly two decades since
she had heaved herself out of the family nest in New Jersey
and moved into the first roach-infested walkup, the one from
which she launched her career.

Until quite recently, just walking around Manhattan at any
time of the day but especially at night in her black clothes,
always black, produced a flutter of joy. She loved the snap of
her boots—expensive, Italian, purchased in Rome, impervious
to snow and ice, square heeled, knee high. She enjoyed every
click of the solid heels on the sidewalk, the sound of the gait
of a confident woman on the avenues.

Now, her lost love for New York was the subtext to her
personal collapse. Slow subways with their interminable waits.
She passed the lame and hungry on her way into lunches and
premieres and parties, and the same smart talk and splendor
that had thrilled her for so many years was bleak and vain. It
was exactly as it had always been but now bared its essence.

After a shot of coffee, the descent into the station. No place to
sit, cling to the pole, crush against bodies. The train screeched
to a halt between 14th and Chambers, and the lights blinked

off. The interior went black. Eyes adjusted to the tiny lights
outside in the nineteenth-century gloom of the rock walls
along the tracks. All the iPhones bleeped simultaneously.
Marjorie's heart always skipped a beat; she couldn't get used
to the sound. She had dim childhood memories of the same
sound from TV screens going blank. "This is a test. Only
a test. If this was a real emergency, you would have been
instructed…"

Passengers shifted, a ripple of unease. The hive mind went
to towers burning, then flipped back as people opened their
phones. It was nothing—phantom emergencies, phantom
fears. The alert was about a missing adult: a woman with
brown hair and green eyes, five foot six, last seen along the
Hudson River near 72nd and Westend Avenue, New York. If
seen, call.

Relief. She peered more closely at the image. *Shit. It could be
me,* she thought. *It could be me.*

She fought back rising claustrophobia by shutting her eyes.
The train jolted, lights flickered back on, and onward they
flew, finally screeching to a stop at South Ferry, the edge
of the island where the Atlantic lapped away at the roots of
global capitalism.

She skipped up the piss-smelling stairs and out into the light.

5. POO PILLS AND AN FBI RAID

Lower Manhattan, 11:11 a.m. Tuesday

Lola Chatterjee, content director, peered through the glass of her corner office with its panopticon view of the *NewsMag* newsroom. Ad buys would be up today. She was wondering if the poo pills would stay down. Before her eyes, a team of men and women in blue FBI windbreakers wandered in and out of the IT room, some pushing carts bearing company servers. Others were going desk to desk, carrying clipboards, counting desktop computers.

Perhaps, she thought, this would be the defining crisis of her career.

The other one would be forgotten.

The story of how Lola Chatterjee, Stanford, Harvard MBA,

had found herself in this dirty business was well known to anyone who followed media news. For a month, two years ago, she had become an unlikely heroine on Breitbart and The Daily Caller and, yes, even Fox News for having famously been pushed out of her last job at an MSM network for failing to observe what the Fox chyrons called "the unwritten rules of woke." Chatterjee had known about her boss's predations. But she was so devoted that she had conspired with him to hire more nubiles, "served up," as the *Daily Beast* media writer put it, "a smorgasbord of fresh tender meat… then ignored and retaliated against women who complained."

A leaked deposition laid a sledgehammer into her career. Soon, she was a poster girl for all traitorous, patriarchy-enabling, female C-suite suits. Friends ghosted. New York Women's Media Foundation and New York Women in Media all quietly cut ties. Columbia Graduate School of Journalism's South Asian Journalist Festival canceled her keynote.

But all was not lost.

To the headhunters for certain other companies, her very public crash was proof of some vital job qualifications: loyalty, discretion, apparently un-woke yet brown-skinned, and a willingness to do anything for the boss. *NewsMag* had offered her the most ridiculously generous package.

It was impossible to turn down. She was reviving a legacy brand. It wasn't part of her portfolio to defend the company against rumors that it was a turning the brand into vehicle for something else, e-commerce scam, money laundering, an influence op for a nationless entity.

According to a *Forbes* headline some time ago, Lola was a pioneer in the SEO game. The off-track betting screens ranking headlines like racehorses, the salary bonuses for beating click quotas, all that was her. If the word *impeach* was trending, she had ten contract writers churning out stories simultaneously with one single goal: to ride the trend. One particularly clever lad had come up with "impeach pie," hauling in tens of thousands of clicks.

She glanced at the rankings: #vegasshooting, #vegasmassacre, #vegas, all hauling in eyeballs.

Ad buys would be up today. It would have been a good day, but it wasn't going to be. Not at all. Lola closed her eyes and reverted to box breathing. The cramp was back. A lifelong stomach disorder had been in full flare for months. Some days, it took every ounce of her energy to hide the pain from her colleagues. Nights were feats of endurance in a fetal position.

Lola had begun her day at dawn, in pain, as she did every morning. She lay still, listening to the distant whirr of the built-in kitchen blender two floors below in their West Village brownstone. She knew exactly what it was: William Roth's probiotically balanced fecal matter was whirring in a bath of some odor-erasing, liquid, sanitizing substance that would leave the good bacteria alive but remove its more offending qualities behind.

Zzzzz! Zzzzz! Zzzzzzzzzzzzz! Then silence.

Dear Will. Dear, dear man. Her pale, heart-healthy husband, a vitamin-slurping, vegetarian investment wizard who studied natural cures as assiduously as he did the small print on *FT* and *Barrons*. He had done his research into her malady and discovered poo pills. That very morning, he had produced his first batch. The theory was that some people had good gut flora and others didn't, and those with good gut flora could donate theirs to the afflicted, like donating a kidney, but with a kit that you could buy from a lab in Cambridge.

Now, before sunrise, this gentle math genius, Samurai in finance, whose brilliance had earned him and his investors billions, who struck fear into colleagues and opponents alike, was in the designer galley clad in laboratory-inappropriate (but at least white) Armani robe she'd given him for Christmas. And now he was very carefully transferring the resulting liquid, metamorphosed into a minty pharmaceutical aqua, no longer brown, into ten capsules—five for his beloved wife to down with a morning smoothie he would make for her next. Five for later.

And Lola would down them all because she had trusted dear Will almost since the day they met as eighteen-year-olds at Stanford—and she was desperate.

Doctors were no use. Will had worried that even the two dogs, Shih Tzus named Abercrombie and Kent, were showing signs of contact stress. A veterinary therapist who made house calls prescribed Xanax for the dogs.

She was willing to try anything. But the irony didn't escape her. She'd ingested her first dose of poo pills on the very day that she walked into a shitstorm in the office.

Lola watched the FBI raid the office she nominally oversaw, crafting a speech for the individuals—thumbs on recording devices and social media feeds—she'd soon summon to the conference room.

Given what she did and didn't know about the company that paid her salary, she wanted to believe this particular shit storm could be just a spring rain. However, it could be a shit hurricane or a shit typhoon.

. . . .

Marjorie Dubois ran her pass against the sensor beside the elevator and waited for a car to descend to the first floor. The card and sensor were the second layer of security. The first was the surly human guard at the desk who insisted, no matter how many times anyone walked past his desk, to see a building pass.

It had been sixteen years since the attacks. Muslims were locked up all over America, and there was a Muslim ban on the ones who hadn't gotten into America yet. Paranoia had spawned its own economic sector, from the exploding security guard population in New York to the dozens of new mirror-clad high rises around Washington, DC.

It was conceivable the building still housed some of the money gods who *did* believe they needed to worry about socialists and Antifa and Occupy. But most of the big funds had moved to Jersey, and the media had colonized the old financial district. As far as this building was concerned, security guards needed to check ID cards every day because newsmaggots were fired daily. Who could predict which ones would return to exact revenge?

There was a third layer of security up on the twentieth floor. An eye in the wall, a small white ball containing a tiny camera. Marjorie stared into it and heard the snick.

She strolled past the hall of empty offices and dusty piled office chairs still wrapped in plastic. The place was vastly underpopulated; the lease of all this excess space was a mystery. Stupendous views of New York Harbor were squandered, and the offices of the ghost corporate executives had never been occupied. She then passed the dreaded HR suite where the firings happened. Finally, the "library" with its banker boxes of bound volumes of the storied *NewsMag* in its glory days going back seventy-five years. No one would ever open them; the Smithsonian didn't even want them.

At the end of the hall was a great room with a grand view and floor-to-ceiling windows on three sides: the East River, the Battery, and the harbor with the maritime panorama of freighters and ferries leaving their great wakes. To the west were nineteenth-century cornices and copper roofs of the old banks, red brick and Maine blue stone. From certain angles, looking between these relics, there peeked the silver sliver of the World Trade Center, mirroring clouds, a time-traveling starship crafted of some non-earth metal, a UFO lost in the middle of the old world.

Marjorie scanned the room. Something was off. Seats were vacant where the worker bees would be hunched, silent, and engrossed in their online content delivery. Vera must be holding an afternoon meeting.

Then, Marjorie saw them—her colleagues. The newsmaggots, as they sometimes called themselves, were not in an editorial meeting but huddled in a corner by the east windows, snickering, thick as thieves. Something about this conclave suggested subversion.

Brickett, the hot cop reporter, waved her over.

"Yo, Marj. We're being raided," he said. The group around him laughed at the word or her expression—or all of it.

"What do you mean?"

"Look." He gestured with his head toward a long blue glass wall behind which lived the IT staff in refrigerated quarantine. Men in blue jackets with "FBI" emblazoned on the back were moving around inside the lair. Another was strolling casually through the general office area, moving down the aisles of reporter and editor stations, carrying a clipboard, and making notes of equipment serial numbers.

So, this was the corporate apocalypse, Marjorie thought, as all their phones bleeped with the same text message. Lola Chatterjee was calling an all-hands staff meeting in the main conference room to commence now.

The group snickered its way down the carpeted hall, leaving the sky and New York Harbor behind, and crowded into a windowless meeting room. Lola stood at the head of the long oval table in an Anne Klein executive black suit with black hair pulled back in a tight bun and electric-blue round designer glasses perched on her nose. Marjorie nodded to her but got no response. She had a complicated relationship with Lola. They tolerated each other, repressing deep distrust. Marjorie caught the eye of the sleeve-tattooed managing editor Vera, an ally, who shook her head almost imperceptibly and returned her eyes to her phone.

Everyone in the room had eyes on a phone. The raid was already trending on Twitter. Some of the staff were getting called from former colleagues at Buzzfeed, CNN, and other outlets.

"Phones off, please," Lola spoke. She waited while the group went through the motions.

"So, I first want to say that this meeting is off the record. I want to remind you of the NDAs in our employment contracts. If anyone in the media calls, refer them to Mark," she began, then nodded to Mark Jarrett, the in-house publicist seated to her left. He was barely thirty, just promoted from social media to replace an older hand.

"And he'll take it from there."

A small round of covert eye-rolls. That horse was out of the barn, dozens of newsmaggots in the same room, all inclined to love and discuss chaos.

Marjorie looked at Lola and, for the hundredth time in the two years she'd known her, tried and failed to suss out whether she believed anything she said or had somehow shut down that part of her human self that needed to do that.

"The next thing, and again, off the record," the content director continued. "The company has done nothing wrong. We have complied with every request the US Attorney's Office has made for documents since this investigation started a year ago."

An audible reaction. That was news—an *investigation*! What, when, who, how, why? More rustling under the desk and against the walls, as people flicked their phones to record.

"As all of you know, the details of an active investigation aren't public, and we can't get into them here. But let me assure everyone here that New Media Inc. is committed to keeping this brand alive. We will maintain our tradition of speaking truth to power. Nothing—especially not this harassment—will deter us.

"So, let's all go back to our desks and back to work. If any investigators stop by your desk, I'm told they're only doing inventory. You are to comply with their requests, but we would ask you not to engage in any conversations with them without our lawyer present. That's it for now."

Brickett, the hot cop reporter, was the first to speak.

"Okay, wait. Where is our lawyer? Where is Alex?" Alexander was the part-time, cut-rate, in-house counsel who vetted sensitive articles. Bald, tubby, sixty, divorced, battered by loneliness, long dirty fingernails, soup-flecked-tie, Alexander Ross wasn't on scene in their hour of need.

"Alexander isn't handling this," Lola replied. "The company has retained Mazurskey and Schmidt. Their team is on their way over now."

"It's already on CNN!" one of the reporters against the wall yelled out. This wasn't news to anyone who'd been scrolling through the feeds for the last five minutes, but perhaps it was to Lola. She paused, looked down at her notes, and then looked back up. Marjorie detected a twitch in the smooth brown marble temple, barely perceptible.

The machine is glitching, she thought.

"Yes," Lola replied. "Yes, and Mark and the team are on it. Let's all get back to work now. And thank you for remembering the NDAs. They're still in full force and legally binding."

Lola rose and strolled out, followed by "the team" of PR kid Mark and some of the nameless suits who lived in the bank of corporate offices and whom Marjorie had never met, whose duties were a mystery to all. Now, she looked at them for the first time and realized that knowing those duties probably should have mattered to her before today.

Marjorie had a flash of déjà vu: a different place with the same feeling. Almost a year ago, at 3:00 a.m. in a sea of red hats in a ballroom at the New York Hilton, the president-elect, a large man, jaw-jutting, goose-stepped around a stage. Shocked celebrants toasted the dawn of a new day, the taste of revenge on their tongues.

This spectacle had a tiny bit of the same intoxicating flavor. Getting up close to holy hell, disaster, a coup, a battle, the collapse of a nation, wondering if the military was on the side of the dictator or the people. Some journalists were addicted to that thrill.

6. DIE ON THIS HILL

Vera watched Lola Chatterjee walk out of the room. She knew the content director well enough—had *studied* her, actually—to understand that Lola was rattled to the roots of her neat chignon. That she remained a pillar of ice didn't fool Vera. The staff wandered back to the newsroom, buzzing with the craziness of it but worried, emailing resumes in expectation of imminent job loss.

Vera slipped back into her office. She was sure of two things.

One, her suspicions about the entity that paid her salary were confirmed.

Two, she was going to die on this hill.

Very few people—and no one in the office—had seen her even slightly annoyed, let alone enraged. Everyone counted on her poise and friendliness. No disaster was too much for her. Vera never lost her cool. She wouldn't today. She didn't get mad or get even.

She just *solved*.

Perhaps it was genetic. The only child of two surgeons, she was born the same year as the first test tube baby and the year the first woman was nominated to the Supreme Court. She was smack dab in the middle of Millennials, two months older than Ivanka Trump and the same age as Beyoncé and Serena Wiliams. Expensively educated and the only brown girl in the Horace Mann class of '99, she had even met Ivanka once at one of the lavish bar mitzvahs all the New York preppy kids got invited to when everyone was thirteen and in braces.

Her parents, teachers, college counselors, fellow students, and everyone had expected her to attend law school. She had the brains for deductive reasoning, logic, and winning debates, a practically photographic memory, and the temperament of a judge. But it turned out she was drawn to a dirtier and more unpredictable life.

Epochal events stirred her soul like a lover.

She turned twenty the day before the 9/11 attacks. The first jet hit while she sat in a modern European history lecture on the campus in New Brunswick. Then came the second one. Class dismissed. She could neither see nor smell the smoke but was seized with an urge to be in the city, on the edge of it. She ran out to her car and gunned it up to Weehawken in half an hour. From the water's edge, she watched the black smoke billow eastward until night fell.

People were crying, and she was never more certain of how she would live.

When she graduated, she moved to an apartment on the Upper East Side, on the twentieth floor of a tower. Family money meant she had never lived in a Bushwick share. If people thought she did, she let them believe what they wanted. No one could guess her background. She dressed without much care, a uniform chosen for comfort, not style.

Life might have been different in a different body, but she was comfortable in her skin. She didn't believe in diets and got enough exercise walking to and from the trains. She was mostly solitary—not anti-social and not lonely. She had one love in college, requited briefly, recalled now as snapshots of long early spring walks, herself rendered nearly mute by a lovely face in profile, then over, the same year. Cher wailed, *Do you believe in life after love?*

And yes, Vera did. She was in no hurry.

Vera had few illusions about the future of the profession, though. She wouldn't be Christiane Amanpour, and no Scud Stud was on the horizon. Behind the calm surface was a ferocious and maybe naive devotion to the profession's ideal.

Speak truth to power.

Sitting in her glass box with a view of the newsroom tense with rumors and FBI agents, she considered her options. Vera's phone was pinging, message after message. She scrolled down, ignored the ones from the media reporters, and saw that Brickett was text-bombing her. She looked over at him: headset on, back in the zone, typing notes, working that

#vegasmassacre story. She texted him, saw him look down, then up and over at her, and nod. He flashed five fingers at her.

Text: "I've got a hot Vegas update." Flame emoji.

Vera no longer cared about #vegasshooting. The horror of it, the tragedy, yes, it bothered her. The hashtag, the clicks, no. She watched the worker bees back at their desks. Some were speaking on phones, a rare sight, with, she was sure, CNN or Beast, feeding them tidbits from the Lola Chatterjee conference. Others had merely hit send on their recordings of the meeting. Audio of Chatterjee's comments was already being uploaded to Twitter by Mick Fink, a Daily Beast media reporter. Scanning all the Buzzfeed rejects and former interns among her charges, Vera wasn't surprised. All were actively seeking a better-paying job anywhere else. None could have resisted the opportunity to prove their usefulness from inside this epic media spectacle.

7. A BROKEN CLOCK

Lower Manhattan, 1:00 p.m. Tuesday

The blue FBI windbreakers were still moving around inside the IT room. Vera had a notion of what they were looking for. A few months prior, a recently sacked investigative reporter had taken up a new hobby: investigating his last employer.

Ted Eisen was like all the veteran scribes who'd washed up at the company—well along on the downhill side of his glory days. Vera had not been sorry to see him out, but she knew it was a nail in his career coffin, if not his actual pine box as well.

Eisen was a loner, like all of his kind. He drank. He had devoted decades of his life and his eyesight to studying the fine print on SEC rulings, legal documents, and FOIAs. He had been obscured behind leaning towers of documents for years.

In his prime, Eisen had been feared. He finally met his watch in a vengeful billionaire who had got tired of his hounding. The man's lawyers had cracked him. They filed a libel suit. Then, they located and put his birth father—a homeless alcoholic whom he, an adoptee from birth, had never met before—on the stand to prove he was unfit.

Which, it turned out, after enduring that afternoon in court, Eisen was. He emerged a few months later on a soft, blossom-scented June day from the sliding glass doors of Rockland Psychiatric Hospital. He had regained the ability to write sentences but had lost the focus his craft required. He was destined to rely on the kindness of former editors and colleagues.

Vera's former boss, who'd known Eisen in his prime, had not hired Eisen out of pity. He had faith in his old friend's potential rehabilitation and his bloodhound investigative skills. Chatterjee had ejected both OGs at the same time during the first of her now-regular restructurings.

Before that, Vera tried getting Eisen to hone in on just one project. For example, he had the goods on Trump's Atlantic City mafia ties. He knew a lot about Trump and had been on him for decades. "Try that," she implored him. "We can publish that." But he couldn't get his head out of this space where everything was *connected*. He could not write until he had all the threads tied together: rogue commercial builders, the NYPD union, the FBI, hedge funders, Israel, Russia, the mafia, cheap Chinese cement, the military industrials, and on it went.

Vera would wake up at dawn and see that he'd been sending updates since 2:00 a.m. They were rambling streams of consciousness from some dying ember in his once brilliantly organized brain. Missives like this:

> *It could be a Forest Gump of a suicidal man who has been given the raw end of every social and health and wealth and family ties…. He gets up every day not knowing if he will make it to dusk, and while he is stumbling through this life, he meets everybody from Prince to Presidents, and he sees what severely dysfunctional people they are and their dark side in the few minutes or hours he spends with them …*

> *Like Donny Junior at Perl Champagne Bar, we go from a near fight to telling our tales of depression and suicide after football concussions… How, after the pre-Super Bowl concert, Trump was so rude and manic, then I caught him in the Hard Rock elevator going up, lol high buying bags of Opioids so he could go home and share them with Melania. We know how that ended… Robert Mercer and Kellyanne and how the security guards warned me, unlike David Koch. He was the real deal, and do not screw with him; he had killed people and is hooked into the Asian mob.*

Nuts—but a broken clock was right two times a day. Eisen knew how and where to look.

After Chatterjee sacked him, Eisen finally cleaned up—or actually got his shit too together in the other direction. He went manic. He rediscovered single-minded focus. He dove into the task with the old fury for justice. He called all his sources at the Manhattan Southern District US Attorney's office. He reverted to a bloodhound but on the trail of what? He thought he smelled the biggest whale of his career: online commerce scam, international money laundering, a felonious octopus.

According to Eisen, *Newsmag's* new owners embarked on some kind of scheme, using the legacy brand as a cover and buying loads of servers and computers. Shell companies led to other shells to shells within shells, oysters within conchs within snails. Fake online storefronts sold monogrammed disposable diapers, finger puppet toys, anti-snoring mouth devices, silicone pads for the insides of bras and retinol skin cream, plastic vampire teeth, Korean eyelash cream, and Malaysian "the world's best bamboo door mats."

Eisen would need a subpoena to get to the real owners.

She'd filed Eisen's latest rambles into the folder on her desktop where the rest of his uncheckable theories lived. For a moment, it occurred to her that he might have instigated the raid. Was he that mad, in both senses of the word? Quite possibly.

Brickett—tall, bearded, Montana born and bred, hot as ever—walked in. "I've got some new stuff on Meadows," he said excitedly. "He had a pilot's license, owned two planes, and had more past addresses than my PI friend has ever seen on an Accutrack file. I want to own this."

Vera clicked on her screen and glanced at a *Washington Post* #vegasshooting update.

"Brickett, I hate to break it to you, but the planes, the pilot's license, and the addresses are already up on the *Wapo* site. Don't you have their feed locked in?"

She watched him blush behind his beard. An excitable boy. She wondered, not for the first time, how long he'd last in the business. It was clear that he loved it but equally clear that he didn't possess the cunning the job he wanted to do required.

Then again, he was a man, and lesser talents were promoted for that reason alone. Brickett was married, and his wife was pregnant. They had just bought a place in Hoboken. They had a small dog that he talked about a lot. Vera gave him five years in journalism before he took a marketing gig at ESPN.

Maybe he'd take an early out.

"I have an opportunity for you," she started. "I need to move you off Vegas just for a few hours. I need someone to help me investigate the company. We're going to break this story."

Brickett laughed.

"Wait, what? Walk me off the worst mass shooting in American history to commit employment suicide? I'm not seeing the upside."

"There is an upside," she said. "First, if the company survives—and I'm telling you that I have reason to think it will not, and we all will be posting our clips on Gigeconjobs.com next week—I'll have your back and promote you to senior writer."

She knew this to be an effective goad. Brickett had complained for months that he worked twice as hard as some of the senior writers who were allowed to travel around the world like Hemingway, blow off meetings, never subject to clickbait quotas, and got paid more—he believed a lot more.

He was right about that.

"If you break this and the company goes down, the profession will hail you as a hero. You'll get another job offer."

The words came out of her mouth even though she knew they weren't true. Whether or not they heroically broke their employers' story and busted their company, as it were, they were tainted by association. They were newsmaggots. Trash-branded. Few would get interviewed for the coveted prestige jobs. None would be hired—ever. The FBI raid only iced that cake.

She saw him waver for a second—*senior writer*—then shake his head.

"Sorry, Vera, sorry. I gotta stick with my gut here. I've got good sourcing in Vegas. I lived out there, remember? I can't help you on this."

"Even if the company shuts down tomorrow?" she said.

He blinked, looked at her, and considered.

"I can't believe that's gonna happen," he said. "Chatter-Flee seemed pretty confident. And anyway, I'll have the story of the year if I stay on this."

Vera accepted defeat. Next.

Vera looked out at the newsroom. Young heads bent over listicles and aggregated supervolcano and asteroid stories. She would not accept defeat. Next.

8. MORE UNREQUITED LOVE AND A PLAN

Lower Manhattan, 1:11 p.m., Tuesday

Vera scanned the room. She spotted Marjorie DuBois, the Lois Lane of the War on Terror. Somewhere along the way, Marjorie had fallen for her own PR—too many *Vogue* and *Vanity Fair* photo shoots, too much fawning in articles, and too many celebrity friends. No more down and dirty. Her copy didn't even come in clean. She needed editors. She was checked out.

Like all the olds hired by *NewsMag*, Marjorie's reputation was a little tarnished. That made them affordable. A few years prior, *The Atlantic* had had to retract one of her stories: no backup for quotes about an American general's involvement in sex trafficking in Afghanistan. It was a high-profile mess. They took her off the masthead.

Marjorie had flung a black cashmere coat over the back of her chair, and it and a Moroccan lamb muffler fell to the floor. It was very Marjorie not to care about the expensive stuff she had acquired—or to appear not to. She had bothered to come in today, which was unusual. Vera wondered for a half-second if perhaps Marjorie had been tipped to the raid and strolled downtown just for the circus. It was more likely she had a lunch date in the area.

Vera had complicated feelings about Marjorie. One part of her, the part that had fallen for the Scud Stud, was in awe of Marjorie DuBois. Marjorie was everything Vera would never be by dint of having been born short, round, and a few decades too late. The golden era of post-Watergate journalism had ended in online splinters, echo chambers of clickbait and disinformation. Despite all her style and confidence, Vera sensed something broken inside Marjorie. Or anyway, that was what Vera *felt* when she thought about—as she did sometimes at home—what it would be like to peel off those black boots of hers and grovel at her feet.

Vera, known to no one, was in love.

She picked up her phone and texted Marjorie. She watched beyond the glass wall as the beautiful pale face looked up, winked, and waved.

"Give me a minute," she mouthed.

Vera sat perfectly still, centered, and waited.

Marjorie knocked before pulling open the door and settled on the couch across from Vera's desk. Up close, she looked tired, with dark circles under her eyes. Strung out. She had

a signature scent, faint and expensive, a barely there waft
of beeswax and paper. Vera felt undone. The object of her
adoration was oblivious.

Marjorie liked Vera. She knew her as a trustworthy,
dependable younger woman in the inexplicably ugly uniform
of Chinatown rubber shoes and tie-dye yoga pants, the
manager who ran interference with lawyers and bosses, who
generously approved expenses. She was a kind of assistant,
even though Vera was her superior on the company hierarchy.

She could fire her but never would.

"Weird day," Marjorie said. She clearly thought Vera was
going to explain everything.

"Yup."

"What's it all about?"

"I'm not sure, something about money, I would guess." Vera
paused, shored up. "Umm, yes, definitely something about
money. So, here's the deal: I have a little project on the QT.
Would you be interested in taking an assignment?" Another
pause. "Investigating a company?"

Marjorie didn't laugh. She just squinted at Vera then down at
her phone and back up.

"A company—as in ours? What makes you think I can do it
better than CNN or *The Times*? Their media reporters have
been texting me all morning."

"Well, I have some leads for you, like real leads that would put
you weeks ahead of the competition."

Marjorie laughed. "Us? Us against us?"

"Are you interested?"

"I'd have to know a little more." Marjorie looked at Vera and saw that she was serious. "Well, I can't say I'm not curious."

Vera proceeded to lay out what Eisen had been doing. Marjorie knew Eisen; she had sometimes asked for his help finding a document. The guy was one of those wizards—crazy wizards.

"He thinks it's a shell game that ends in Bitcoin or something." She proceeded to lay it out: a cult, a corporation, unrelated businesses, ending with a weird property purchase in Plattsburgh, NY.

When Vera stopped talking, Marjorie had a little smile on her face. Half amusement, half adrenaline. The urge to mischief that animates some journalists.

"Well," Marjorie sighed. "Deep well."

"Yup."

"You plan to publish this?"

"With verification."

"Who's going to lawyer it? Alexander seems AWOL."

"Haven't thought that far ahead."

"That doesn't seem like you," Marjorie said.

The comment hit Vera with a tiny dart of heat and hope. If Marjorie DuBois paid enough attention to her to know what was "like" her…

"Well, I'll find us a lawyer," Vera said. "It won't be a problem. Of course, there will be other problems."

"Like losing my paycheck and health insurance, maybe?"

"True." Vera let that sit there; it could go either way.

Marjorie had one of the last *cushy* jobs in the business. Her byline entitled her to orders of magnitude and a higher salary than the worker bees. However, her output was slim, and her duties unclear; she was known to leave town whenever she felt the urge and had spent whole weeks in Mexico or France. She was the definition of phoning it in.

She was widely resented; younger colleagues pretended not to see her in the halls.

It couldn't possibly last.

Vera watched her. Her human radar was on target, as it often was. Marjorie was going to be willing to commit job suicide.

A corporate suicide bomber.

"Ahh, fuck it," Marjorie said. "Give me Eisen's stuff."

9. THOUGHTS AND PRAYERS

Above Las Vegas, 1:00 p.m Tuesday

Nevada terra firma slammed his economy seat. Puffs of sand and tumbleweed spun past, and the sere landscape, rippling with heat and blurry with speed, came into focus. Brakes screeched. Full stop.

McCarran International Airport was barely five miles from the crime scene. The police would find that the shooter had aimed at the fuel tanks along the perimeter and just missed—a bullet propelled five miles, nearly a bullseye. Someone had been having fun with guns.

Passengers were already up and laughing at the flight attendants talking about waiting until the plane came to a complete stop before pulling down their bags. Many were soused on four flying hours' consumption of tiny vodka bottles in cans of V8. They stumbled and laughed and sat back down.

The Strip had become the worst gun massacre crime scene in American history, and twenty-four hours later, the show would go on. Goodman thought, *I'll have a vodka tonic with a dash of thoughts and prayers.*

The dry wasteland outside the jet's porthole took him back, back, back—twenty-seven years, more than a quarter century—to Operations Desert Storm and Desert Shield, a camp at the Kuwait-Iraq border. He had years of intimacy with powerful guns and other weapons that didn't require an ounce of human strength to kill, just electricity, 20/20 vision, and a joystick.

He landed in Kuwait at thirty. A working-class patriotic stud in his prime. Three generations of Brooklyn Irish firemen on his paternal side, and a dozen veterans of US wars going back to the Spanish-American War on his mother's side. Ribbons, medals, metal mess kits, and old wool uniforms were boxed in the attic in the brownstone, a building now worth millions of dollars, sadly no longer in the family.

Back in the day, he could bench press with the best Dominican boxers in the gym. At thirty, he still had the ripped body of a Trojan warrior, now turned to fat, redhead turned silvery. Some women liked his large, long-lashed baby blues that looked capable of tears. They either fell hard for those strangely feminine eyes, so out of sync with the hard body, or were left cold. There was no in-between.

Goodman could divide his fifty-five years into roughly two halves. From birth to thirty-one, Goodman was a patriot. In kindergarten, he had asked that his birthday cupcakes be frosted red, white, and blue. The family hung the flag outside every national holiday, including Easter Day. He enlisted, and he fought. He walked the talk.

Iraq had cost him that certainty and set him adrift.

He joined the Army straight out of two wasted, in every sense of the word, years of college (Fordham, criminal justice, blown scholarship, barely cared). He eventually got his shit back together. The military did it for him. It turned out he had a knack for languages. After a few years at Mannheim, he was moved to the Defense Intelligence Agency.

When Saddam started moving the Revolutionary Guard toward the Kuwaiti border in the spring of 1991, the US commenced the biggest buildup since World War II. For its part, the DIA deployed eleven National Military Intelligence Support Teams (NMISTs) to, in military lingo, "directly interface with tactical commanders in the field." NMIST interrogators harvested what the war college analysts would eventually call "highly perishable data" in civilian vernacular: sort prisoners, ID the high-value ones, interrogate, relay intel, rinse, and repeat.

Goodman was one of these team leaders. The NMIST teams linked commanders in the field with the national intelligence community. His job had been questioning defectors and POWs. Defectors were a valuable source of intelligence regarding Iraqi capabilities and intentions. No one spoke Arabic, so they relied on local translators and teachers hauled in from Jordan and Saudi Arabia.

For three months, Goodman worked the desert cells in the enemy prisoner-of-war camps as they filled with Iraqi soldiers and officers. Most had turned themselves in. They ran like rabbits from American bombers, leaving the incinerated remains of comrades in the sand, indistinguishable from their boots. Survivors stripped and walked into the field, hands up. If the smoke and fire didn't get them first, they were cuffed and brought to the cages.

Goodman and his colleagues were expected to pony up fast on the lost art of questioning with and through interpreters. Interrogations like that had not been conducted since Vietnam. The gray heads who remembered how it was done were few and far between.

Goodman got pretty good at it, sharing cigarettes, waiting patiently, his strangely girlish blue eyes disarming the quivering mustachioed defectors, his bulk and glare eliciting answers from the reluctant. He might have been one of the men Colin Powell was talking about when he told Congress later, "No combat commander has ever had as full and complete a view of his adversary as did our field commanders in Iraq."

They gave him medals.

But then Goodman got sick. Depleted uranium shells? Too much time with prisoners in the greasy smoke of the burning oil fields? No one knew or ever would. Long before he returned to the Land of the Free, he was weak and wheezing, sometimes bedridden, limbs on fire, crippled with diarrhea. On bad days, he started to believe protecting Gulf royal families had nothing to do with American national security— and had not been worth his health.

On his last days in Iraq, he went to the Al Rasheed Hotel in Baghdad. Barely hanging on, he was wheezing, eyes bloodshot. The belt of his pants was buckled to the third new hole he had skewered himself, fifty pounds off his frame, shit out in three months.

He had come to the five-star hotel for a final meeting with a Ba'ath Party informant. He was looking forward to a C-4 flight and a German-made goose down comforter in Mannheim.

That afternoon, crossing the hotel lobby, a trio of American and British photojournalists he'd encountered in the field waylaid him. They called themselves The Three Fucketeers. Cleaned up, still high on war, the Fucketeers invited him to one of the Masgouf fish restaurants along the banks of the Tigris that, incredibly, still stood intact across from the rubble of Ba'ath Party buildings, serving wood-roasted, fresh-caught whole Tigris fish on enormous platters.

The Fucketeers had managed to commandeer a case of bootleg Arak and cheap white Bulgarian wine. The dinner party moved back to the Al Rasheed into a suite equipped with more Arak and even some smuggled Kentucky Bourbon and French Armagnac. A gorgeous young woman had been tagging along all night. The Fucketeers treated her like both a goddess and a pal. She had a foul mouth and smoked a lot. From the moment she sat down with them, Goodman was undone. It was hard to look at her. Here was a face that might change him, but he didn't know how. The night ended at dawn in his room, a pink steaming Mesopotamian light pouring in, a green-eyed, voluptuous war zone Venus named Marjorie DuBois beside him.

The girl was a great beauty, even hungover, smelling of cigarettes and booze, sallow, undernourished with eye bags. She carried it with the carelessness of the young. She couldn't have been older than twenty-two, a reckless hellion. She padded barefoot out of his room and down the hall to hers, carrying her dress and shoes in one hand, half draped in a sheet, Amazonian breasts, melon size, real and bare, laughing at his panic and running after her, trying to throw a blanket on her out of respect for the local female customs.

A year passed. VA doctors at Mannheim and then Walter Reed had no answers. There was the suggestion that it might be PTSD. He heard that as "all in your head" and, filled with quiet rage, left the Army.

A nurse he was intermittently dating told him about the Congressional committee investigating what was being called Gulf War syndrome. He signed on as a staff investigator with subpoena power. His point of view changed, like the click in an optometrist's office when the lenses were switched from clear to blurry, to clear again.

He met sick and dying men in wheelchairs, old before their years. He started to see them and himself as meat pawns in a world run by, well, he wasn't sure who ran the place anymore.

He didn't expect to see her again, and he didn't until one afternoon on Capitol Hill three years later. He spotted her in the audience at a contentious hearing with the Defense Secretary about Iraq War sickness. She was older, more glamorous—wild horse corralled in a skirt suit and heels but unbroke. They got re-acquainted over martinis and then more intimately in her hotel room. She was down from New York, working for one of the news magazines. She had a self-promoting aggressive streak that stunned and paralyzed him. It was hard to say no to anything she asked him for.

For the next six months, she popped down to DC often on the northeast corridor Amtrak for martinis and sex, and a little more. Before the committee report was finalized, she published what would be a prize-winning story based on his documents, contacts, and experiences. After that, she was always busy and infrequently answered his calls or emails.

He wasn't exactly blindsided by her abandonment. She was, as he had joked with her often, out of his league.

The committee released its report to the public, heavily edited and redacted. Goodman was devastated. He'd put it all on the line, whistleblowing and talking his buddies into testifying. Nothing was going to happen. No accountability.

He left the Hill staff job around the same time and accepted an offer from a newspaper to cover the Pentagon. He told himself the career move had nothing to do with wanting to be adjacent to her.

He was good at it. He knew liars from truth-tellers and where documents and bodies were buried. There was so much more to understand and reveal. He was no conspiracy theorist. Unlike other investigative journalists, like Ted Eisen, he would not be cracking up. He would not get lost in the labyrinth. He believed in Occam's razor: The most obvious, least-complicated explanations almost always turned out true. That and the fact that he knew all the ways, at least in the military, inefficiency and bad planning explained more than conspiracy theories.

He still retained just enough love of Patria that he was one of the journalists who would still loudly tell anyone listening he considered Ed Snowden to be a fucking traitor.

September 11 and the spectacle of *Shock and Awe* were history now, too. Even ISIS was on the run. The world had moved on, and it certainly appeared to be more of a hellscape than before. All of it was prologue, receding, the time before now. The thing was that you could never stop long enough to understand what just happened. You had to keep your eyes on the road ahead.

Goodman accepted that he would never have all the puzzle pieces behind the oil wars. He had good, strong days when, despite that knowledge, he worked angles anyway. Other days, he despaired and smoked too much weed and too many cigarettes, drank beer on his back porch, and stared at the wall of bamboo—an invasive species taking over suburban DC—that shrouded his yard.

He called those moments "Zero Visibility Possible" after the signs Army logistics had hammered into the yellowish crust of earth over the sea of oil in southern Iraq to warn grunt truck drivers of roads susceptible to blackout dust storms.

One time, he'd found himself inside one of those blackouts near Basra. He was in a car with two subjects on a bomb-blasted strip of asphalt that Saddam had laid over miles of a flat, cracked brown crust of earth above lakes of crude. First, it was just a yellow shadow on the horizon, then brown, rolling across the sky toward him, the driver/translator, and the prisoners. Daylight turned to night—a stifling lightlessness, a darkness that was not night but more terrifying, impenetrable by flashlight or headlight.

The driver had pulled over to wait. He'd seen the unseeable before. They sat inside the car; Goodman was fighting off claustrophobia. There was howling outside; inside, their high-level detainee muttered prayers in Arabic.

Hours passed before the blindness lifted.

Goodman still carried inside him a piece of that dark and sudden helplessness. It no longer pierced him with panic. It was his situational awareness.

He did not despair. He just waited for it to pass. He accepted that he might turn up nothing more than a puzzle piece, a clue for others who came later, centuries later, maybe.

Assembling the record was enough. It had to be.

He kept a quote inside a frame on his desk from *Moby Dick* by Melville: "For small erections may be finished by their first architects; grand ones, true ones, ever leave the copestone to posterity. God keep me from ever completing anything."

Like that book's hero, on good days, Goodman believed he was pursuing something noble and elusive, harpoon in fist.

Even if the white back of truth was never in his sights.

10. #VEGASSTRONG

McCarran Airport, 1:11 p.m. Tuesday

Goodman waited in his seat as the drunk passengers staggered up the aisle. He had his laptop open and squinted at the "William Meadows" image in the old ex-agent's newsletter group photo.

It could be, couldn't be, he thought. An agency public information officer had already emailed a denial to him: not the same Bill Meadows, no record of that guy in the CIA. He promised to send a birthdate to back it up. Goodman didn't know how the press attaché could be so sure. He knew *why* he would have to sound sure, of course.

He flicked away from the image and scanned news updates. The death count was up to fifty-nine in Vegas, with more than eight hundred injured. *Jesus. War zone numbers,* he thought.

Not even.

The shooter was dead, self-inflicted gunshot wound to the head, clean. Cops had taken credit for the kill earlier. Now, they were saying Meadows had done it himself, just put one of his twenty-nine guns in his mouth and blown off the top of his head.

Other news: The shooter had a "roommate," a woman. The FBI was in the process of retrieving her from Malaysia, where she'd been in the process of buying a new house for her family. Meadows had transferred the money for it to her in large tranches to a bank account in Bangkok only a month ago. No. She don't know where the money came from. And she had not asked him why he had sent her back to her family.

The incuriosity suggested a beaten woman or one who knew how not to get beaten. Ask me no questions, bitch. Goodman wished he could interview her himself. He bet the cops would get nothing.

He checked his phone for updates. The mayor, the chief of LVPD, and a spokesman for the FBI would be on the Strip in an hour. Pete, a DIA buddy from his Iraq days who did investigations for the LVPD, would meet him there, too.

The revelers were out of the aisles, whooping into the jetway. Goodman rose to pull down his bag, and black dots popped into his peripheral vision. He clutched the edge of the luggage container and looked down to steady his dizziness. He knew from long experience that he had gone alarmingly white, and he kept his face down to avoid attracting concern. Years on and off corticosteroids had slowed Gulf War Syndrome deterioration. The cure left its own trail of damage in his body. Vasovagal episodes were nothing to worry about, the VA medic assured him. He squeezed his eyes shut and felt the full weight of time and gravity pressing down hard on his 230 pounds. Sometimes, when this happened, his knees buckled, and he woke up on the floor with people kneeling over him— not today. He forced his head back up, breathed, and went clear again.

McCarran airport was tense compared to the mood inside the plane as it bounced west. There were terror-squad quartets, baby-faced National Guardsmen and women in camo, another level of protection—maybe military or Vegas PD SWAT—in bulletproof black, mirror wraparounds with their thumbs on automatic weapons. A few leashed German shepherds twitched on their haunches. ISIS had claimed responsibility for last night. Bill Meadows didn't strike Goodman as that kind of convert, but he knew law enforcement rarely missed an opportunity to eyeball ragheads in airports.

Passing the Guardsmen, Goodman felt their youth and how much he remembered that they could not.

He made his way toward the arrivals hall, where a large black-and-white banner was hung below the "Welcome to Sin City" mural.

#VEGASSTRONG

Okay, he thought, so it would be like that: hashtag, name-your-city-strong, and some thoughts and prayers. That, as usual, would have to do for "closure."

He felt a surge of the old rage. The adrenalin cleared his head of the remnants of the vasovagal episode.

Out the automatic revolving doors and into the oven, the sky
was a taunt, joyous, borderless blue. White concrete sparkled,
blinding new arrivals from the cloudy zones. He shaded his
eyes and hailed a cab. Pulling out of the airport, they passed
a giant American flag flying at half-staff. The cabbie had
the radio tuned to local news, sound bites of the President's
"thoughts and prayers, we condemn the evil" speech were
on a loop, interrupted by traffic, weather, and the announcer
urging listeners to join a "Stop the Bleed" campaign, reeling
off addresses where they could give blood.

The announcer threw to a reporter on the Strip: "Police say
that for ten minutes, Bill Meadows unleashed a relentless
barrage of more than eleven hundred high-velocity rifle
rounds into the audience gathered thirty-two floors below
him. The gunfire had already ceased when the tactical team
came to his door. It took the team a full hour to bust into
the suite, only to find Meadows dead. Authorities are still
searching for answers."

The cab pulled up a few blocks from the Strip, as close
as possible for a car. Police and military still swarmed the
area. The Luxor, with its ersatz pyramid, obelisk, and palm
trees, lay in front of him. The Mandalay Bay was to the left,
completely off-limits to the press for the moment. Neon
cowboy boots, slot machines, and outlines of dancing girls
kicking up their heels still blinked down the Strip. Everything
was gilt—a gaudy, winking adult playpen of cheap cement,
glass, and steel, glitter still aglitter. Of course, the show would
go on. The revelers in the plane from Washington would
expect to get what they had paid for—an all-inclusive trip of
dreams, including Blackjack, cigars, Scotch, girls, and steaks.
Some gamblers might even consider having so narrowly
missed the massacre as one of those signs of good luck bettors

looked out for, like the rabbit's foot, four-leaf clover, the purple sock, or the red tie.

The taxi dropped him off at a line of TV trucks sprouting satellite dishes on tall masts. A pack of journalists milled around, flipping notebooks, talking into their phones, and, Goodman knew, trading rumors and updates. The Strip and its concert venues were cordoned off with yellow crime-scene tape. The no-go zone was visible, a vast area still littered with white surgical gloves, white tents, numbered tarps, and small dayglo flags marking out evidence—bits of flesh, shoes, clothing, blood, and bullets, he reckoned. Forensic experts in paper suits and hair nets moved among the flags, kneeling and taking pictures.

Goodman angled toward rows of folding chairs set up for the media. The sun was fierce. He needed to sit down. A cop in dress uniform took the mic.

"This is an active crime scene behind us, so please take your seats," he started. "We have a few updates for you, and we won't be taking questions at this time." He looked down at a note and back at the reporters. "Weapons: We can confirm the suspect acquired his weapons legally. In the last five months, Mr. Meadows purchased fifty-five weapons, most rifles, to complement an existing arsenal of twenty-nine guns. Accomplices: Based on what we know now, the suspect acted alone. We recovered four laptop computers from the suspect's room. Forensics are examining them now. Some of you have asked about ISIS; we are aware of the rumor that a foreign group has taken credit. We do not rule out terrorism, but we have no evidence to that effect at this time."

Goodman looked at the men and women lined up near the podium: uniformed cops, the mayor, representatives from the FBI, and men in suits; there were at least a dozen people. There was also a Congresswoman. Most were not there to speak. He didn't wonder why they came. He imagined there were quite a few more offstage, ticked off because they hadn't been invited up. Few public events attracted the eyeballs this one would.

His phone pinged. Pete texted that he was about fifty feet behind him and suggested they meet behind the TV trucks. Goodman squeezed past the row of knees, feeling clumsy. He was standing beside Pete before he even recognized him. In contrast to Goodman, Pete had gotten lean and scrawny over the past quarter century. His skin was leathered from decades in the desert. They shook hands, and Pete handed him a fat yellow envelope bulging with printouts. *Old school,* Goodman thought as he took it. The kids at *NewsMag* would have demanded an email instead of this pile of dead trees.

"Guy's had more addresses than I've seen in twenty years in the business," Pete said. "You'll see. I ran the Accutrack for you. And I got you some of the early police documents. I like to give the slow, old guys like you a head start." Pete was in a hurry, something about an illegal parking spot, so they parted ways, agreeing to meet for coffee sometime when Goodman's deadline lifted—in another few decades.

The mayor was speaking, but Goodman had no interest. What mattered was getting up to speed on the contents of the envelope. He scanned the vicinity for the nearest air-conditioned lobby and headed for the Luxor's faux ceremonial steps and Pharaonic glass doors.

11. TWENTY-FIRST CENTURY WARFARE

Washington, DC, 3:00 p.m. Tuesday

The press corps is gathered in the Rose Garden, tiny, muted
figures milling about on the screen of his laptop. CNN logo.
Waiting for the President. Silver refreshes the Twitter feed
on his phone with his right thumb, eating the last savory
bits of last night's Pad Thai with the fingers of his left hand.
The scene on and around his desk is one of chaos and filthy
wreckage, crusty old takeout cartons, coffee spills dried on
the pages of briefing papers in no particular order, tangles of
cables and wires, dirty socks and underwear.

Preston Silver had covered four US Presidents, but he had
only hung framed photos of himself with three of them on
his home office wall. Those three artifacts joined the framed
history degree magna cum laude, Princeton 1986, and framed

covers of his two books about the 1996 and 2000 elections, along with some of their better reviews. The newsprint was yellowing. The honor remained.

There was a bright-white square on the same wall, which had been, until recently, occupied by a photo of him in a suit and tie, standing beside his now-ex-wife, the legendary feminist political strategist turned politician, Allison Silver, in the Senate chamber on the day she was sworn in as junior US Senator from the great state of Maine. Their marriage, birthed in the back of a campaign bus in pre-2000 America, rocky from its earliest days, went full shipwreck during Mrs. Silver's campaign. One of Preston's side-women decided that a Senatorial contest was as good a time as any for revenge and went public with emails and pictures. Silver had intended to "stand by" his spouse, whose family fortune he'd got quite happily accustomed to living with. But Senator Silver, putting her money where her mouth was on the "woman needs man like a fish needs a bicycle" adage, commenced divorce proceedings two days after her swearing-in.

The mess was wrapped up in a month, with such blinding speed that he was still dizzy. The daughter they had raised together since she was born in 2000 had not spoken to him for a year.

Silver was a bit of a wreck. He was not exactly down for the count but was still nursing his wounds.

He still has his title, White House correspondent, albeit attached now to a derelict legacy media enterprise publishing journalism in name only. He has worked out of his home office for almost two years now. He has come around to practicing the lazy email interviewing and copy-and-paste reporting he once scorned as kid stuff. The revelation that he could do it all from the kitchen table in his boxer shorts had changed his dining and grooming habits. He hasn't bothered to trim his fingernails lately, and his shirts are often food-stained when he does venture out.

He still does don his signature bowtie on the rare amble from DuPont Circle down to the bunker on Pennsylvania Avenue. The traditional attire helps him nail the occasional interview among the men and women he regarded, albeit only to himself, as repugnant reactionaries and fascists.

Such forays are infrequent now for several reasons. Besides his personal disaster, his professional cachet—the reason that MSNBC and sometimes even the Sunday morning shows booked him—had been eradicated in a single night. He'd been dead wrong in November 2016, clinging to bad numbers on TV until the dawn of the day after. That was embarrassing but survivable. Who didn't make such mistakes?

But going into the White House press room now meant running into a gauntlet of younger reporters who have openly reviled him since the morning he woke up three months ago and saw 50,000 Retweets of a one-sentence Tweet addressed to him that read, "You have been reported for targeted racism and harassment." His eyes adjusted to the reason long before his brain did: He had recklessly Tweeted Thomas Jefferson on free speech just before the Charlottesville Nazi march. The fact that his Tweet had nothing to do with C-ville was irrelevant. He was tagged as a white man aligned with the slaveholders and their statues.

Finally, another reason, one too embarrassing for him to admit even to himself, he avoids the White House because he is physically afraid of some of the current President's men. He's quite sure their swaggering machismo is real, and he doesn't want a punch in the face.

Silver had been late to comprehend the degree to which so many Americans lived in rage and panic. All that time on campaign buses, all those stops in Des Moines, Sioux Falls, Manchester, Columbia, and Columbus, and all those sweaty gatherings. How had he missed it? Sure, he'd interviewed Birchers and KKK sympathizers. But he flicked off the recording and looked around for other interviews as soon as he realized what they were about. They'd been right about the media elites; he literally did not see them.

At this hour, he had, of course, heard about the raid on *NewsMag's* HQ up in Manhattan. Two of his former campaign bus colleagues at *The Times* and CNN have texted him, "WTF?" They had no time for him before, and now, for a story, he was their best friend. He hated that he would do the same in their shoes.

Silver could give zero *effs* about what went on in New York. The place could burn down. He routinely muted the morning meetings. If Vera or one of the editors remembered he existed as their White House correspondent, he could turn around a copy-and-pasted aggregation in fifteen minutes.

That *NewsMag* HQ was possibly also a crime scene was just another twist on his dizzying professional downward spiral. He was no longer in denial about his career. He knew where it ended for him and could sense the abyss sucking him in. He had only one viable plan to save himself. It involved replacing Senator Silver with another wife as rapidly as possible.

The President has arrived at the podium. Silver flicks the sound back on. Truth be told, he would rather be working on another story that didn't require him to look at the President.

He was in the middle of writing about how small-town librarians in West Virginia were being trained in using Narcan. When he first heard about this, it had moved him deeply. But as with every interest he'd mustered lately, this one fizzled. He had on his screen a half-written piece, which needed many more interviews. He had emailed several city officials in Harpers Ferry but had never heard back. He couldn't bring himself to call and speak to them. He had jotted down a few notes for the article, toying with a headline that amused him.

Come for the opioid antagonists; stay for the Shakespeare.

He rests his eyes on the livestream of the oaf behind the podium with the Presidential seal. The speech isn't bad, considering the man is believed to be dyslexic and unable to read a teleprompter. He's hitting all the churchly, patriotic notes: God, Bible, flag, rinse and repeat. He hadn't veered off script for a second. Of course, there would not be a word about gun control and the madness of allowing a private citizen to amass an arsenal large enough to conquer a small Central American capital, pack it into twenty pieces of luggage, heave guns and ammo onto a bellhop's luggage cart, and have said bellhop—Hispanic for sure—roll it into his room.

It had taken five or more trips. Silver thought about how the shooter must have tipped the bellhop.

"Scripture teaches us the Lord is close to the brokenhearted and saves those who are crushed in spirit," the President said.

There was a slight breeze; the papers on the podium stirred. Why did the cretin even carry papers around? Were they optics props? But the president's amazing hairdo held solid. "We seek comfort in those words, for we know that God lives in the hearts of those who grieve. To the wounded who are now recovering in hospitals, we are praying for your full and speedy recovery and pledge our support from this day forward.

"In memory of the fallen, I have directed that our great flag be flown at half-staff. I will be visiting Las Vegas on Wednesday to meet with law enforcement, first responders, and the families of the victims. In moments of tragedy and horror, America comes together as one. And it always has."

Now come the thoughts and prayers, Silver thought, *3, 2, 1…*

"Melania and I are praying for every American who has been hurt, wounded, or lost the ones they loved so dearly in this terrible, terrible attack. We pray for the entire nation to find unity and peace and for the day when evil is banished, and the innocent are safe from hatred and fear."

Silver licked the last of the peanut sauce off the lid of the take-out container. This was a fine speech, although it lacked the incendiary element, the insult tricked out as comedy, the borderline defamatory statement, the racist dog whistle, that had become the gold standard for any *Newsmag* political story.

He thought of Lola and how he loathed her and her bounty for clicks. This speech wouldn't cut it alone. Vera would not post it without something more from him. He sighed. He really ought to try to get an interview. This was, after all, looking to be the highest kill-count gun massacre in American history.

He ran a greasy finger over the WH Contacts list on his phone and scrolled down to one: Ferenc Folkus. Fox News' favorite Hungarian emigre was a belligerent unrepentant fascist who proudly advertised his membership in an organization with roots in an actual Hitler-loving political organization. Folkus routinely got into shoving and screaming matches with reporters at rallies, on the street—didn't even matter if they were male or female—and at restaurants and on Capitol Hill. These YouTubed incidents had made him a bit of a hero.

Folkus' policy positions included hanging abortion doctors and jailing journalists who "insulted" the President. He had imported straight into the American capital a brawling political style more commonly seen in footage of the Moldovan Parliament. He had pioneered the publicity shot with an AR15, the now politically obligatory campaign portrait for many. But when he slugged a *Times* Congressional reporter outside the Senate chamber while flinging an anti-Semitic slur at him, Senior Advisor Folkus' White House career officially ended. However, he was still on Fox a lot and, therefore, had a direct line into the Big Guy's amygdala.

The badge of shame Silver wore for his Tweet-alleged racism and his high-profile dumping by the Gloria Steinem of the US Senate gave him a sliver of an advantage over his reporting colleagues with the current regime. Some White House insiders who loathed the lamestream media took his calls and chattered away, believing—and he didn't correct them—that he might have converted to their side.

Silver keyed up Folkus and hit call. After one ring, it went to voice mail. Silver knew Folkus, like all White House staff, preferred encrypted chat platforms. He switched over to Signal and stabbed in a quick message.

Preston Silver: *Hello. Hope you're well. Do you have a few minutes to talk about how the team is handling the Vegas situation? BG is fine. I'd like to include your take.*

He hit send and waited. Ten minutes passed while he scanned his Tinder feed. A smorgasbord. He was revving up a text flirtation with a redheaded thirty-six-year-old Georgetown assistant professor of international relations when the Signal app lit up on his phone.

Apparently, the Hungarian bull was feeling a bit penned in. Maybe none of the cable bookers had reached out to him for a hit today. Folkus had uploaded a screed:

You may attribute this to a White House insider:

The radical left will use this terrible event as an excuse to crack down on lawful gun owners. You heard it from me first. This is likely a Deep State, leftist Democratic Party op in concert with mainstream and corporate media that has ramped up "kill the white people." They believe their own propaganda and are hysterics, and they are out for full-spectrum dominance. This is twenty-first century warfare! You carry out the attack and then blame your enemies who you have just killed. They carry out the attack, cover it up, and blame us—lawful gun owners.

False flag! Get it? GUN-GRAB! They are going to false flag even bigger now. They're going for broke to break our will. It's only a matter of time before these Communists put fifty million people into forced labor camps. I'm not kidding. They're coming. You wanted to see the fight for America, you're living it, 2017, right now! Toe-to-toe combat with the globalists, politically and on the battlefield.

The message ended with links to a 4chan message board thread that identified Meadows as a registered Democrat, and to two other dubious news sources that were popular, Silver knew, with conservatives and the alt-right. All repeated that Meadows was a Hillary Clinton supporter and included a picture of him or someone who looked a lot like him in a pussy hat. Folkus also included a link to the Russian news agency Sputnik reporting the FBI had identified the shooter as a member of an Antifa-linked terrorist group, and a link to an Infowars YouTube clip with Alex Jones suggesting Meadows was part of the same covert black ops CIA team behind 9/11.

Twenty-first century psyops warfare. Designed to disarm conservative Christians.

Toe to toe with the globalists.

Silver thought about that for a while. Then, he sat down and wrote about the President's speech, including the unnamed White House insider's take. Headline: "Conspiracy theories about #Vegasshooting grip Washington." And subhead "False flag?" He was about to hit send when he decided to add another bit of bait: #gungrab?

With that flourish, he hit send on his piece. The tattooed lesbian—he was sure of it—Vera and the soul-dead careerist Lola would love the clickety-clicks on this one. Hopefully, he thought, it would count as sufficient effort, and he could walk away for the week.

Now, back to his priorities: Tinder and the final arrangements for tonight's date. He commenced a Google search on Dr. Jill Maitland Matthews. Knowledge was power. A few image search clicks indicated the Tinder photo was not digitally improved. She was just as hot in the video clips of her lectures and in an evening dress in society shots of Washington philanthropic events. And what else: Could there be another Jill Maitland Matthews on the "40 Under 40" list? He thought not! She was moneyed Diplo-royalty: Her father descended from steel barons and a former ambassador to post-Soviet Estonia, her mother from the mainline Philly branch of the Maitlands, a signer of the Declaration of Independence in her DNA.

Maybe his luck had finally turned.

12. CLAIRSENTIENT BEINGS

Lower Manhattan, 3:00 p.m. Tuesday

Marjorie Dubois, noise-cancelling headphones on and head bent into Ted Eisen's crazy file, hadn't looked up in an hour.

When she'd accepted the *NewsMag* position, she had heard the rumors about the cult behind the eighth reboot of the legacy brand. But the offered salary was substantial. She had reasoned with herself that a religious order could be no worse than Rupert Murdoch's operation in terms of sketchiness. And wasn't the history of journalism in America also the history of robber barons and corporations trying to buy a piece of the public's mind? What else were Hearst and Jay Gould and McCormick?

As far as she knew, the owners had never once been involved with the editorial decision-making. That had made it easy to put concerns about them out of mind. She had taken the salary and skated along, enjoying the slick office, travel, and very limited demands on her time. She was aware that she had been brought on as one of a few show ponies, along with Silver and maybe Goodman, to add a varnish of legitimacy to the operation. An "award-winning journalist" for the masthead. She was living on borrowed time in that regard, resting on her laurels and not doing much to earn a new crown. Every day, she loosened further, grew a little less rigorous, and moved further away from the ambitious person who had won prizes.

Now, arrayed on her desk was one of the many matters she had avoided: the truth about the people who paid her bills.

The Temple of the Emissaries of The True Divine Light Chiropraxis officially had two centers: one in Los Angeles and one in the Mojave Desert. Crazy California. Where the nuts rolled. The religious order was not a product of 1970s acidhead revelation. It was relatively old by American cult standards, founded in the 1850s by followers of an itinerant seer named Thelma Birdsong. Birdsong had preached, mostly west of the Mississippi, that to enter the higher kingdom, the self must receive, in her neologism, "clairsentiently" delivered teachings. Her followers believed her teachings cleansed and purified through *scientific* prayer, and they practiced renunciation of carnal beliefs and meditation. So far, so good, but by this cleansing, not bodily death, one escaped the cycle of reincarnation in the material world and the law of cause and effect.

Thelma's heirs, four generations of Birdsongs, had been the Temple's prophets for a century and a half, concluding with the current Grand Leader, the very ancient Alphaeus Jackson Birdsong, who would leave no bodily heirs. Under his leadership, in the 2000s, the L.A. temples were modernized, and the order built a new Sanctuary East as a retreat complex outside Plattsburgh, New York. The new headquarters was a corporate park with a glass and steel ten-story tower in the center. The Temple operated as a business but was run as a tax-exempt church with a new logo, "TDLC" coiled into the claws of a rampant eagle in profile. Birdsong and his followers had also instituted "schools" in various cities.

Marjorie pitied any California-bred clairsentient missionaries dispatched to proselytize on the Arctic border of upper New York. She read on.

It was clear from the expansion that TDLC had come into some serious money around 2000. Who, what, and why were the questions that had obsessed Eisen. He had meticulously combed SEC records and pulled up dozens of LLCs associated with the TDLC corporation.

NewsMag's parent company, New Media Incorporated, had been organized in 2012, after which TDLC had embarked on a frenzy of limited liability incarnations. Dozens of LLCs existed and shared—surprise!—the same address where Marjorie and a staff of busy newsmaggots were now beavering away, 800 John Street, New York, with FBI agents still turning over machines in the IT room.

Eisen's file also included news clippings of stories about TDLC's special tax exemptions, granted by the city of Plattsburgh and the county where the newest school was being built. There was a photo of the aged Birdsong in a business suit and hard hat and in a wheelchair at the groundbreaking on the site of a derelict lumber mill last year. The mayor had hailed the deal for bringing construction and hotel jobs to the areas.

Her leg cramped. Marjorie realized she hadn't uncoiled for a very long time. She stood up, stretched, and walked to the tiny office kitchen, rummaged around in a cupboard for a tea bag, and waited two and a half minutes for the microwave to boil a cup of water. The three-minute ding coincided with a tiny rumble from her phone on the counter. She watched it quiver four, five, six times, then stop. A final ding let her know she had a voicemail. She dipped her tea bag in the steaming cup and waited for the water to turn brown before she picked up the phone. The possibility was always there.

One in ten, one in twenty.

It was him. A text popped onscreen: an eggplant. Instant physiological response. Heat and juice. She picked up the device and her tea and walked back to her desk. She took a few burning sips and let herself feel the thrill of this moment of his attention. Whatever he had to say, it wouldn't satiate her desire. She knew that by now, but she listened to the voicemail. His California surfer boy drawl, keyed midway between tenor and bass, poured over her like warm syrup.

"Hey, what's up? I'm in the city tonight. Thought we could… Sorry I've been out of touch. Uhh, can I make it up to you? Call me."

The ball. In her court. Ever so briefly. It was up to her now to decide how long she could hold back, how long to let herself imagine him wondering where she was or whether she still cared, all the while knowing that he knew he had her pinned, and if she didn't reply, he had, at a stroke of his thumb, numberless possible girls in every port, the port of New York City's list among the longest.

13. HIGH ON WATERMELON MOUNTAIN

Lower Manhattan, 4 p.m. Tuesday

Marjorie had never been the kind of journalist who felt ethically compelled to maintain a strict separation between sex and sources. The way she saw it, women were hobbled by their exclusion from the men's networks in finance, the military, and now the world of algorithms. Sex was a way to level up, a tool. Maybe a little more complicated than the simpler tools of the trade, the laptop or recording app, but a tool, nonetheless. Fortunately, she liked it, too. Her deployments in the realm of the sheets were rare and discreet enough that editors had never confronted her, but much as they might have suspected, the material was always too good. She knew her competitors talked about her unethical ways. Occasional seduction for a story was a piece of her legend.

It worked when she was in control.

She needed Steve Burns both in bed and as a source. He knew things about surveillance, new technology, and private security contractors. He was inside on all the shady business Snowden had revealed.

Oh, he hated Snowden.

The Watermelon Mountain National Weapons Lab deposited a biweekly check in his bank account. A few generations ago, his predecessors at the lab had invented and refined atomic weapons. The lab was a cog in one of the original American military-industrial giants, a company that had been around since before they were born. An aviation giant had spun off from jets and missiles into nukes and myriad subdivisions, including "communications" and even cadres of mercenary contractors, without which the US military could not effectively wage the oil wars.

His specialty was *networks*. He had access to the keys of the supposedly encrypted corners of the worldwide web. One night, a few weeks after they had met, he became Facebook friends with every contact she had in Lebanon, Jordan, and Syria. When she asked him about it, he laughed and told her she could be a spy.

He insisted that the friending frenzy was coincidental and benign. Maybe that was true: Who among her contacts wouldn't want to be Facebook friends with a white-hat cyber warrior? But then he started showing up in her passwords.

He assured her it was all coincidence. Although she knew it couldn't be, she let his gaslighting soothe her.

She understood too late that the sexy science geek was not what he seemed. She was on one of the government watch lists from all her trips into ISIS territory. The watch lists were vast, obscure, and assembled by machines or machine-people.

She couldn't be sure what he was. But through some alchemy, distrust transformed into helpless lust. Love rendered her passive. She was more abject than every other citizen of the world whose digital footprints and phone calls he reduced to packets and sorted into threat levels.

By the time she knew what he was really up to, he had permeated her communications—her networks in addition to her body. And she didn't even care.

She knew something, though, a fact that helped her retain a shred of self-respect. He was afraid. He feared the people and places she had been. He was crouched before the terrorists. Like so many, he had been unmanned by 9/11. He still traveled the world and crossed borders entitled by an American passport, and his tall, white, and confident American manhood, but always with a little fear stuffed deep in his pocket. She'd seen it, felt it. Assurance of her superior courage sustained her. It was all she had against him in the battle for power that was one of the twin engines fueling her obsession.

Her phone pinged again. A text.

"Ignoring me?"

She couldn't help herself.

"Of course not! Busy day here."

"I heard... " he replied.

She let that sit, and he texted again a minute later.

"You probably need to relax. I want to help.... Peninsula, Room 320."

She could feel the heat rising. Yeah. Okay.

"Roger that."

"I CAN roger that!" Another eggplant.

As usual, her almost sated lust was both distracting and intensely focusing. Now that she knew where he was and that she would see him soon, her sense of control returned; she could work with greater clarity and speed.

The definition of sanity is the ability to love and work. Old misogynist Freud might be right about that. So, she had these moments of sanity.

She returned to Eisen's folder. The groundbreaking on the TDLC outpost in Plattsburgh had happened a year ago. Eisen had appended a news clipping about a groundbreaking on a bitcoin farm in the same city and how these farms might use more electricity than some nations.

Bitcoin. Blockchain. She dimly recalled that the Newsmag had been at the forefront of covering this new kind of money a few years prior. At the time it had seemed to her like more clickbait for Wall Street bros, or a lure for tech advertisers. A quick web search turned up recent news stories about a sudden surge in value. Bitcoin was "taking off," "poised to explode."

Was it possible there was a connection between these developments and Plattsburgh the appearance of federal agents in the office? She went back into Eisen's file, and saw that in his last pages of notes he'd scrawled out a kind of map, drawing connections between TDLC, New Media Inc., Plattsburgh, and a long list of offshore banking experts.

She looked up Plattsburgh on a map. She checked the time, still afternoon.
She could conceivably drive up there in six hours. A wild feeling rushed through her body. It had been a long while since she'd experienced the physical sensation of news, of being on the trail of discovering and exposing something nefarious. It was not better than sex, but related, certainly.

Plattsburgh or Room 320 in the Peninsula?

It was verging on 4:00 p.m. She could conceivably drive up there in six hours. Plattsburgh or Room 320 in the Peninsula? A wild feeling rushed through her body.

One could do both—love and work. A kind of insane sanity.

She grabbed her coat, shoved her laptop in her bag, and headed out. On her way to the elevator, she glanced at one of the flat screens tuned to NY1. They were running that picture of the missing woman again: a woman in black clothes with brown hair and green eyes. The scroll below said: "MISSING. Have you seen this individual? Please call NYPD."

Marjorie peered up at the screen. *Jesus. It could be me,* she thought.

14. HE WAS GENTLE; HE WAS SICK

Las Vegas, 2 p.m., Tuesday

Christopher Goodman skirted the crime scene tape and strolled across the asphalt ribbon shimmering in midday. The chemically maintained grass glowed an unreal tropical green at the edge of the Luxor. He went up the ceremonial staircase, designed to resemble the ancient steps up which sun-god pharaohs climbed to their thrones. Two doormen in Egyptian tunics offered to help him with his duffel bag, but he declined. The air was deliciously cool. The *zing* and *bing* of the video poker games added a crazy rhythm to the thump of Drake singing "One Dance" on hidden speakers in the cavernous casino.

Goodman found his way to the bar and slid into a booth at a table shining like a black mirror. A waitress in a Cleopatra head-dress and revealing version of the statuary tunic on the doormen sallied over. She gave him a smirk when he ordered a hot tea. Behind her, he saw the bartender creating elaborate Bloody Marys in jumbo goblets, each with a celery stalk the size of a saxophone and a colossal shrimp on a punji stick.

The first sheet of paper inside Pete's envelope was a printout of an address search. Pete had been right about it. Goodman had never seen a current residence list like it: some twenty-five addresses in Southern California and New Mexico.

What the hell?

The cops had run Meadows' recent credit card purchases. A week ago, he'd purchased five thousand rounds of ammunition from a private seller outside Reno. Legally. He bought some prescriptions, some gloves, and a lot of sushi. He also stopped at a Walmart the day before the shooting to buy plastic flowers, a vase, and a styrofoam ball. Something for someone to remember him by? Or for his grave?

Next was a sheaf with a cover page marked "EVIDENCE: From the Vista suite at the Mandalay Bay." Police had collected twenty-five guns, four laptop computers—one with child porn on it and all with searches for outdoor concert venues dating back to the summer. A long blue plastic tube with a snorkel mouthpiece was found stretched across the floor of the room with the broken window. It ended at a black plastic funnel.

Goodman looked at the picture of the weird rig. DIY tear gas protection? But this guy had easy access to all the latest military gadgets. He could have bought himself a mint gas mask along with the ammo. No. This was something. Dennis Hopper's huffing in *Blue Velvet* came to mind.

A bottle of diazepam 10 mg with Meadows's name on the prescription and two inhalers were lined up neatly on the bathroom vanity. Two pairs of black gloves were laid neatly side by side, one pair in each of the two adjoining rooms of the suite.

According to the Mandalay Bay manager, Meadows had checked in exactly seven days before the massacre. The manager recognized him right away; he was a gold member. He might have forgotten about the check-in, except that Meadows argued with the desk clerk. The reservations desk had put him in the west-facing Vista suite and on the wrong floor. Meadows was adamant: He needed the suite on Floor 32, which had to be facing east, out over the Strip.

That was quickly sorted out. The manager stepped in; this was a VIP guest. Meadows then made several trips to the parking garage, returning with an unusual amount of luggage—some twenty suitcases. Meadows personally oversaw the transfer. Grainy screen grabs from the Mandalay Bay parking and elevator cameras showed the back of a balding man in a business suit with a piled luggage trolley and a bellhop.

According to hotel records and video surveillance footage, for four straight nights before the massacre, Meadows had been a nocturnal animal, perched glassy eyed at a few video poker machines for fourteen hours straight from 4:00 p.m. to 6:00

a.m. A few hours after dawn each day, he would retreat to his room and order sushi to be delivered.

The sushi chefs in the Mandalay Bay kitchen knew him by name because he often sent whole platters back to be redone—at 9:00 a.m.

There was more from the manager's preliminary statement: "Shortly after checking in a week ago, Meadows had demanded that his room be cleaned immediately with natural cleaning products because he couldn't bear the smell of the chemical cleaning fluids. He told the desk that he had a condition doctors could not diagnose and that chemical smells everywhere gave him migraines. He could not get away from them."

The police interviewed one of Mandalay Bay's housekeepers, who was dispatched to try to fix the problem. She recalled the man standing in a corner while she scrubbed the room down with water and his natural cleaner. He didn't speak and never took his eyes off her, not for a second. No, she hadn't noticed any weapons, just his blue eyes on her. *El Diablo*, she told the police. She'd seen the devil.

The Mandalay Bay manager had something else to share: He had worked previously at Caesars, where Meadows had gained elite seven-star loyalty status. But he lost it when the casino realized he had learned how to game out Ten Play Dollar and Double Bonus Poker. Until then, Caesars had rewarded him with stays in the presidential suite with its own pool. When he was told he was being banned, the normally arrogant and silent Meadows raged at the man. "He was like screaming at me. He went white. And I'm like, that's really kind of rare," the manager said.

Goodman flipped the page, sipped his tea, and rubbed his eyes. The drinkers at the bar were getting loud. The disconnect between their gaiety and the massacre less than twenty-four hours ago was profound. A part of him longed to order two of those tall bloodies and slip into the same cheerful oblivion.

Goodman watched them for a while, then turned back to the packet. His eyes hurt. He rubbed them, squinted a few times, and read on. Another interview.

A twenty-seven-year-old woman identified as Dasha had spent a few days with Meadows at the Mandalay Bay. Goodman was baffled and impressed. Of course, the LVPD had sources in the demimonde of Slavic escorts. She called him "paranoid and obsessive" about 9/11 conspiracy theories, FEMA camps, and how the government was going to start locking up Patriots and gun owners. He had allergies and talked about how he believed the federal government had poisoned him back when he flew planes for some agency.

Dasha had been with Meadows a week ago at Mandalay's sushi restaurant during a meeting with a man who knew how to convert a rifle from semiautomatic to fully automatic. The man wanted to sell him the plans. Meadows would only pay if the man did the conversion for him. The man had declined, saying: "I'm too old to spend the rest of my life in federal prison."

Dasha recalled that Meadows berated the man, "Somebody has to wake up the American public and get them to arm themselves. Sometimes, sacrifices need to be made."

Next page: Police had transcribed a preliminary video statement with Meadows's girlfriend. Sorai Chen had been reached in Malaysia this morning. She was now being escorted back to the States by a US Marshall.

"Ms. Chen reports that Meadows was never violent. He never spoke of killing. He was gentle. He was always sick. She doesn't believe he would do this. He was debilitated with a disorder that he believed doctors couldn't cure. He told her doctors had diagnosed a chemical imbalance. At the beginning of their relationship, he told her that she would have to stop wearing lipstick and perfumes because he was allergic to them. Meadows eventually made her subservient, and their relationship became all business. He had been collecting guns at a rapid pace for the past year. Ms. Chen sometimes accompanied him to shooting ranges. Sometimes, he talked of a government plot to kill him. She never took that seriously. A month ago, he transferred a hundred thousand dollars into a bank account in her name and told her to go back to Thailand and buy a house with it. That's what she was doing when contacted. She has agreed to cooperate fully."

Next page: Meadows' younger brother, Pete, had called the Vegas PD from his home in San Diego as soon as he saw his brother's face on TV. Pete informed the police that his brother was "super smart" and perhaps had done everything in the world he wanted to do. He was bored with everything and maybe just wanted to be known as having the largest casualty count in gun massacre history. Pete told investigators that both he and his brother had far above average IQs and that he was calling in to help and show "how dumb you motherfuckers are," referring to law enforcement. Pete was sure his brother planned the attack methodically and would have needed every item he brought into the room.

Next, an odd page, handwritten. An unnamed inmate at the county jail had been shouting as soon as Meadows's face and name were broadcast. He had to go to the LVPD. A jail guard had faxed the statement, inmate's name blacked out.

Meadows and I were dual VIP players. No blood, no foul. I would say he was Bipolar, manic-depressive like all of us gamblers are. He was always upset he was not on the list to meet celebrities. He was a math geek and obsessed with being part of the Vegas elite. He used to come in the evening, get a big Cuban cigar with a wrapper, and hang out in the middle of the VIP entrance. Then, he would lose his shit when they didn't invite him inside. I told the casino manager he was a ticking time bomb, but money talks and bullshit walks.

I used to call him Bozo the Clown. Remember that clown you used to hit, and it'd come back? That was him. As you know, a lot of the non-tourist regulars use the casino to money launder from rich Asians to Russians to drug dealers to business people just making dirty money.

Anyway, Wynn runs the Hard Rock Casinos. He has the big one in Macau, and Bill almost always cashed $10,000 checks per day at Hard Rock. I was always curious how Wynn knew Meadows. It's unusual for a non-whale, see. Usually, only a $500,000-a-day and up player gets the meet-and-greet from Wynn.

When I got to know him, he started out weird but okay. Then, he would drink and get verbally abusive. He popped pills like Xanax and other mood stabilizers. I remember one day, he showed up in valet with a rental truck. Then, he showed up with fists full of money around 2009, first at the Hollywood Hard Rock and then at the Vegas Hard Rock. He used footballs and whiskey. When they threw him out of Hard Rock, he went on to Caesars. For him to get basically thrown out of Hard Rock was odd. Wynn knew something was going on.

The nameless inmate was clearly nuts or one of those fabulists who showed up around mayhem and disaster and wanted to seem in the know. Still, no stone unturned. Goodman wondered why the jail guard or the LVPD would keep his name off the statement. Probably, Wynn. Associating that name with a mass murderer from a jail cell in Vegas was probably bad for career longevity in this town.

The final item in the folder was Meadows's employment record. Meadows had graduated from Caltech with a math degree but went to work for the US Post Office in the 1980s. Goodman snorted. It was hard to picture this cat delivering mail. He remembered that the CIA cover for spies in the old days had always been the post office. After the USPS, Meadows had worked for the IRS, reviewing defense contracts. In the early 2000s, he worked in the private sector as an accountant at a company called TDLC.

Goodman's tea was cold. He'd been hunched over the papers for so long without moving that his old lumbar disc injury was throbbing. He struggled to stand and stretch and caught the young waitress looking at him with pity.

There was a lot here, but the government jobs most intrigued

Goodman—USPS and IRS defense contract auditor. That was a hell of a position. Maybe a certain kind of man could make a lot of money under the table.

15. AN AFTERNOON TRYST

Peninsula Hotel, 5:00 p.m. Tuesday

It was not quite dark—a cool fall evening, the blue hour end to a sapphire day. Autumn in New York, live it again. She passed the doormen, taking note of their eyes on her. Men could smell a woman in a state of arousal; she was certain of it. Sometimes, in the hours right after she'd been with him, she noticed heads jerking up as she walked by, strangers' eyes locking onto hers across the room. Animal instincts were highly underrated in the modern world. How much unspoken information passed between human beings, unconscious of what their bodies were constantly perceiving.

She considered stopping in the plush dark bar to prolong the anticipation but decided against the $20 beer. There would be plenty of intoxicants in Room 320.

Lochinvar opened the door with his usual expression upon first seeing her again, a combination of sheepish and wolfish— the crooked smile. He was wearing jeans, and his shirt was half tucked in, a white oxford cloth tail draped over one side, jacket and tie draped on a chair, shoes off, a calculated state of super sexy deshabille. She found his two-day stubble beard highly erotic. She knew he worked on it, arranged the untucked shirt and narcissistically groomed the stubble for maximum effect. There were no accidents with this man. He put a lot of time and thought into seduction. That level of deliberation from any other man would have turned her off. Until he came along, she had only known wordless animal sex.

"Hi," he said and reached a hand out to clamp the back of her head and plant his mouth on hers. Their first kiss remained one of the memories she often went back to when they were apart. After hours of walking around Washington together in an increasingly addled and horny state, he had followed her up to her hotel room. He'd pulled out his laptop to show her some pictures and had asked her to open hers. The two laptops sat open on the coffee table as she moved her face closer to his until she was moaning and writhing with his mouth on hers. The kiss had lasted, in memory, maybe an hour. When he finally moved his hand to the outside of the wet underwear between her legs and said, "I could make you come," she was already there. It wasn't until much later that she discovered he had downloaded her entire computer contents wirelessly into a folder on his. By then, she understood that she was too far gone to object.

She mapped the start of her professional disintegration to that kiss. He was surveilling her, and since she could not reject him, she stopped doing things she thought he might want to know about.

Kissing, the delicious giving-in, the submission she lived for. He pulled back and looked into her eyes, still holding her hair.

"Hi."

"Hi."

"What do you think of my boudoir?" he drawled. She noticed the bed was already turned down. There were chocolates and champagne on the bedside table. He had this tendency toward Hallmark card romance. Once, he had strewn rose petals on a bed before she arrived.

She shed her coat and shoes in the doorway and sat on the edge of the bed to pull her dress up over her head. Then she lay back in bra and underwear, a languid odalisque.

"Are you posing?" he said. He was shedding his jeans. She could see the rod poking up and out. "I like that look."

"Pour," she whispered, pointing at the bottle.

"First? Before this?" He moved closer to the head of the bead and pulled down the elastic on his briefs, moving his penis close to her face. Eye to eye with that tool, the sensitive head longer than any she'd seen. Exquisite. She opened her mouth.

An hour of ecstasy later, he did pour for her and himself, too. She used the Peninsula sheets to wipe the sweat and drool off her face and accepted the dainty glass of bubbles.

"Goddamn, you're fucking beautiful," he said. She knew he meant it, even if his flattery wouldn't be enough to sustain her once she stepped out of his room.

"I've got to go upstate," she said. "Tonight."

"What's up?"

"I'm going to Plattsburgh to see what the owners of our company are up to."

"Can I come?"

This was not unusual. They'd done a few other road trips together. Sometimes, he found inexplicable oceans of time for her alone. In retrospect, she knew these travels together always had to do with national security stories. He'd asked to come along on a western road trip and lingered in Cheyenne while she interviewed young Air Force men and women assigned to man the doomsday ICBM capsules planted in the high plains of northern Colorado. He'd driven her to a meeting with a whistle-blowing defense contractor in Leesburg and waited five hours in his car. She'd let him come along because, she had to admit, his penis was now more important to her than source anonymity. So what if he was keeping tabs on her network? If her job helped keep him around for an extra day or two, she could live with it. In fact, it was great.

"Seriously? You'd leave this?" She gestured around the posh digs upholstered in shades of pearl and sand, the fake starlight of midtown Manhattan winking gold and red through the windows, and the platter of charcuterie and caviar on the table. "We'd have to leave now. I want to have a look-see tonight."

"I happen to have a car," he said. "Please let me be your Jimmy."

This was a joke between them. She was Lois Lane; he was her admiring mule, young Jimmy. He drained his glass in a gulp, sat up in the bed, moved his head down her belly, the hank of hair falling over his eyes, and dribbled champagne on her while dragging his fingers lower. "Unless you can't bear to leave."

Swooning again, she focused her eyes on the digital clock on the bedside table: 6:30. They'd be in outbound traffic for the first hour but could make it to Plattsburgh before midnight once they hit the thruway. She rolled away from him and bounced onto the floor.

"Plenty of time for this at a motel if we go now."

He gave her the simultaneously sheepish and wolfish look and pointed down at his erection, then sighed.

"You owe me a Quality Inn fuck, then."

"You know I'm good for it." She was already in the bathroom, yanking a brush through her hair, rinsing her slimy thighs with her free hand.

16. WICKED F. WITCH

Lower Manhattan, 6:00 p.m. Tuesday

"Obviously! Obviously, you can't be serious."

Lola Chatterjee was sitting at her desk, Vera standing before her. Lola had called the young managing editor in for their regular EOD meeting. Usually, they looked at the daily click-through stats and tweaked the headlines, assessing which stories worked and merited another day on social media and which would be better off dead.

Lola had just pulled up the numbers on her screen and was about to run through them when the mild-mannered mistress of equanimity, Vera, erupted.

"Are we seriously going to act like this is just another afternoon at the office?"

Lola raised a perfectly threaded eyebrow. She assessed the younger woman in front of her and, not for the first time, experienced a wave of distaste and astonishment. The shameless adiposity of the girl, a poor thing with her genetics, but still, couldn't she go on a diet of Spirulina smoothies and Adderall for a month like women her age at Condé Nast? The tie-dye yoga pants, advertising—apparently with pride—those hams of thighs. Her surprisingly tiny feet were tucked into cheap Chinatown slippers, bearing all that weight. Ugh!

The content director stilled her loathing. Lola's management training had been so seamlessly installed in her mental operating system that responses to almost every crisis were by the book. It's *not* about you. Company first.

"If you mean, are we going to alter our daily goals over a small legal matter that has nothing to do with our operation, I would have to say no."

"It seems to have everything to do with our operation. The FBI just hauled off half our IT equipment."

"I think you'll find that we can operate fine without the machines they took."

"If that's true, that's weird, and I still think the staff deserves an explanation. Most of them spent the afternoon looking for jobs. They need more reassurance."

The content director sighed. She tapped a manicured nail on her phone, which was flickering with incoming text messages. She was silent for a minute.

"Look, can I be frank with you?"

Vera suppressed a snicker. *No, you can never be frank; you'll always be Lola with me*, she thought.

"First, let's not forget that using company property or company time to search for jobs is a termination violation. And everyone signed an NDA as part of their employment contract—including you. I assume we agree that talking to media reporters about the company is cause for termination."

"Maybe that's why they're already looking for jobs," Vera said. She opened her mouth to say something else, but Lola held up her hand.

"Vera, let me finish. *NewsMag* isn't going anywhere. We've been speaking truth to power for half a century. We have a reputation. We have an obligation to our advertisers. The legal situation won't affect our operation. It will be resolved very, very soon. I need you to be out there." She gestured toward the newsroom and beyond, the gathering dusk over the gray-green waters of New York harbor, before continuing, "out there, motivating the staff, keeping them on board—and keeping the rumors in check."

She looked back at Vera directly into her eyes.

"I know you. You know how to do that. I trust you."

Lola could see Vera weighing this last. She had to hand it to the young woman; for a tattooed tubby, she was remarkably poised. They both knew trust had been absent from the relationship since the day Lola had been brought in to replace the executive editor. Lola's allegiance was to Lola first, the company second, and last to her dogs. Trust wasn't an issue, but Vera still had enough youthful insecurity not to correct her. She would want to be trusted. She didn't even flinch.

"Now, shall we look at the stats? Silver's item on the White House insider's massacre theory won the afternoon. Can we get him to spend a little more time updating it?"

Vera had her notebook out, apparently jotting down Lola's orders. She was aware of the content director's scorn and under-estimation. She would have liked to share the fact that she had a trick or two up her sleeve, too—the fuck-you exit strategy of a cache of emails and documents implicating the execs in numerous instances of fraudulent advertising traffic. It was a civil lawsuit waiting to happen. But she just kept taking notes, except that she was doodling a remarkably true portrait of Lola Chatterjee with fangs, captioned in capital letters: "WICKED FUCKING WITCH."

17. WHAT A LOT OF PEOPLE ARE TALKING ABOUT

Washington, DC, 9:00 p.m. Tuesday

Around 9:00 p.m., Preston Silver's second scoop on the administration's reaction to the #vegasshooting went up on the *NewsMag* site. Silver had cobbled it together with a new interview with another White House insider, even more inside than Ferenc Folkus.

This one was more than happy to be named in the story: Harrison Benson.

Benson was the now-legendary "disruptor" communications strategist. In his 1980s preppy costume of three polo shirts, a button-down oxford, khakis belted with a duck belt, and sailing shoes, the aging boy wonder of the extreme right had weaponized cheap social media ad tech with unlimited millions from one of the most eccentric billionaires in New York. He famously coined the phrase "flood the zone with shit" for spreading misinformation, conspiracy theories, and outright lies to confuse gullible Americans, thereby getting credit for The Boss's upset election.

Benson had spent years skulking in media purgatory, growing more resentful as big-name reporters refused to take him seriously, and Hollywood ignored his self-financed films about the morality of capitalism and the wisdom of Ronald Reagan. He had burned through three wives (two having filed domestic violence charges in their divorce papers). Each of those experiences had increased his conviction to restore women to their natural handmaiden role.

Men, yeah, white men, were *victims*, too. Oh, yes. They just didn't cry and tattle to the nanny state.

Silver and Benson had a cordial relationship dating back to the campaign's beginning. Then, the old rules were still in place, and Silver thought it possible that he might write another book about the election of the first female president. Silver had crafted and published an early story about Benson, the Rebel on the Right, singlehandedly building and gilding the man into myth. That made him an OG in a growing Benson fan club. Benson had an adoring following among some of the top male—nominally liberal—journalists in Washington and New York. They trekked to his DC office, where he entertained with cases of Scotch and Cuban cigars. At the same time, they recorded his exegeses on revolutions, Machiavelli, Lenin, populist uprisings, and smashing the administrative state.

Benson was finally living his dream- to be respected—no, feared—by the crowd that had sneered at him. He was sixty-five and paunchy and getting the last laugh, as the brains behind the dyslexic bull in a China shop leading the Free World. Better late than never, he was a global brand, set for life, with a post White House future already mapped out and lavishly financed. A Milanese industrialist had even funded a think tank under his name headquartered in the family's *Castello* on the Italian-Austrian border. From there, where heirs to the fascists and Nazis had never really given up hope, Benson enjoyed a long season of drinking *Alto Adige* wines, feasting, and strategizing with the global right. When he reappeared in Washington, he had grown out his aging surfer-dude locks and wore his hair brushed back and shoulder length like a blonde Claude Levi-Strauss.

When Vera first Slacked him about Lola's latest request, Silver was inclined to blow it off. He disdained Vera and Lola equally. In practice, though, it felt pretty good to get such a public pat on the back and to watch his reader numbers tick upward into the high six figures—almost a million shares. None of his books had sold more than 20,000 copies. The networks and nodes that profited off the insatiable desire among millions for proof of global conspiracy, had been alerted to his little piece. It was reasonable to think Harrison Benson himself had seen it and would be happy to add his thoughts to the developing story or, Silver corrected himself, *narrative*.

Silver checked the time. He had several hours before meeting his date, the impossibly hot Georgetown professor with the aristo DNA. He needed a shower and a shave, matters lately overlooked, but he could take care of the grooming in a jiffy. He didn't have much hair to comb. He'd have to fish out a clean and pressed shirt; somewhere in the closet, there had to be a full dry cleaning bag, although he couldn't remember the last time he had brought his shirts in.

He opened the phone and scrolled down to Benson's contact card. The guy now had six active numbers with LA, DC, Maryland, and Virginia area codes plus an international number—a lot of phones. Silver also had Benson's proton mail address because Benson intended to avoid the nanny state's records preservation act.

Silver decided to start with the DC number. He was slightly shocked when Benson picked right up after one ring.

"Brother Silver, how's life, my man?"

"Uh, hey, good. No complaints here."

"I see the deep state got into your headquarters today. What's that all about?"

Silver had a nanosecond to react. Share rumors or play dumb.

"I don't really know. Not a good look, but I'm sure they'll sort it out."

"I hear it's about crypto."

"Don't know anything about it."

"Okay… Well, what can I do for you and the dying legacy media brand today? You've got life support on the line here."

The Mid-Atlantic bray, the frat-boy laugh. Silver checked his irritation. Sucking it up and forging ahead were primary tools of the newsgathering trade.

"I'm just looking for your take on the Vegas shooting. I talked to Ferenc this morning and…"

"Stop right there! I saw your piece. I'm happy to assist. You're on the right track. The others seem to be missing it."

"Missing what?"

Silver was fiddling with his phone, trying to start the recording app. Benson waited; he knew exactly what was up. *Beep*, the recording started.

"Missing what?" Silver said again. "Talk to me."

"Oh, where to start? The Masonic theory? I'm not saying I agree with this, but maybe, bear with me, okay? Ever since 9/11, there's been this theory about the history and symbolism of two pillars falling. Two towers, undeniably, lead to Masons. So, some people say that 9/11 was engineered by the global elite, which, as you know, are Masons, historically anti-Christian, anti-church. This is *Egyptian Book of the Dead* stuff, right? So, 9/11 was a sign, a Masonic Satanic symbol aimed at raising the underworld."

Silver groaned reflexively. Benson chuckled.

"I'm not saying I *agree*. Just sharing what I hear a lot. It's no accident this Vegas shooting was staged beside the Luxor Casino Resort, the great glass pyramid, right next to two shafts of light. Folks are saying it's all part of some crazy plot to bring about the actual end of the world. The final solution. Fear, control."

Staged. Silver could not tell whether Benson was serious or not. Flooding the zone with shit. He muted his skepticism.

"Well, I hadn't heard about that."

"No, you wouldn't. I wouldn't expect you to. But that's because, my man, you are not reading the signs. You are not taking the actual activities of blood-drinking, baby-eating, elite pedo-libs seriously. You are still writing the script for the wall of illusion, blue pill reality, dude. I'm not saying I *believe* any of it, myself. I'm just sharing with you what a lot of people are talking about and believe. You know, our *deplorables.*"

Silver knew about blue pills. He appreciated the reminder because he would want to pop one in his jacket pocket for tonight. He wrote down "blue pill" on a fresh notebook page, tore it off, and laid it in the middle of the kitchen table, shoving away empty takeout boxes to clear a space around it. This was important.

He also knew *The Matrix* and Pizzagate. Benson was winding him up on that.

"Okay, Masonic world domination may be obvious to the red-pilled crowd, and that's great. But, umm, it will take a little more time than I have to track that down. Can you give me something I can use tonight? What does Harrison Benson really think about the Vegas shooting?"

"Well, I'm hearing it was a false flag and that they've deployed the crisis actors again. Like, the victims were paid actors employed by George Soros—some kind of globalist PSYOP. Like, there's this guy Donald McMann from British Columbia, from *Canada*," Benson sneered the word, "who supposedly caught a bullet in the back of his head that only grazed his skull and knocked him down. He's giving interviews, describing how happy he and his girlfriend are to be alive and how fortunate they feel. Well, go to his Facebook page now and check the comments thread. Pull it up; I'll wait."

Silver booted up Facebook and searched for Donald McMann of British Columbia. Immediately, a long thread of vile, misspelled comments accusing the couple and their families of being paid liars.

"Obviously a TERRIBLE CRISIS ACTOR," wrote one woman calling herself Veronica. "HE'S SCAMMING THE PUBLIC. This was a government setup."

"YOUR [sic] A LIAR AND FILTHY PIECE OF CRAP," wrote another named Karen.

"You'll pay on the other side," said a user named Mitch.

The thread went on for hundreds of lines: "LYING BASTARD," "scumbag govt actor," and "fucking FRAUD."

A Facebooker called TheRealAlexa had posted, "I hope someone comes after you and literally beats the living fuck outa you."

Gold.

Silver was already cutting and pasting when Benson weighed back in. "You see it? Okay, at least a million people agree with them, maybe more like 50 million. We have the data. These people are legion, my man. You can't keep ignoring them."

"Uhh, yeah, okay. How do you know these Facebook posters are real people, not Russian bots? "

"How do *you even* know the supposed victims are real people?

Were you there? And even if you were there, could you prove to me that was real blood, and those were real bullets?"

"Oh, come on, man, facts are facts. Some things are verifiable."

"Uh, let me stop you right there. That's what you don't get. See, what you call facts don't matter anymore. They haven't for quite a while, actually. That happened when you weren't looking. The fog of war crept up around you, man. Information PSYOPs are twenty-first century warfare. You should see what deep fake technology can do. The Speaker of the House is fucking a horse on a livestream, and you won't be able to tell the difference. Go, look. I dare you!"

The fog of war. Twenty-first century PSYOPs. Silver marveled, not for the first time, at how this crowd's messaging moved in lockstep like they had some "words of the day" or a topic rundown emailed to them every morning.

Whatever. Silver arranged the horrendous comments thread into a story file. He hated to admit it, but this crypto-neo-Nazi with his European *philosophe* haircut, recent recipient of tens of millions of dollars in untraceable dark money now probably stashed in Turks and Caicos, money that came along with probably a whole lot of fresh tail, was right. The clickbait that Lola demanded lived or died in the virtual world of social media, crawling with influencers, trolls, and bots that could amplify or crush his byline, no, his career. "Reported for racist harassment" was tattooed on his reputation.

And he wasn't going to forget it.

It took Preston Silver barely twenty minutes to file a new story with Harrison Benson's speculations about the deep state conspiracy and its crisis actors and the global Masonic long game against Christians and capitalism.

Headline: "White House strategist won't discount rumors about #vegasshooting: Benson sees Masonic conspiracy, globalists, and deep state."

He hit send, then went to take his first shower in a week. He still had half an hour to locate a fresh shirt and Uber himself over to the bar at the Four Seasons in Georgetown—plenty of time.

18. AN EROTIC RIDE TO BITCOIN

New York Thruway, Rather Late Tuesday

The drive up the New York thruway had been an erotic excursion, one for the New York State Highway Department's history books. Marjorie had kept her lover unzipped and in a state of semi-to-full erection for the first ninety minutes, using her hands and mouth while he drove. When he couldn't take it anymore, somewhere around Poughkeepsie, with northbound Quebecois semi-trailer trucks honking and veering around them in the passing lane, she had held the steering wheel while he jerked off in the direction of her bent head. Then he'd managed to keep driving, quite fast, with one hand on the wheel while he pleasured her from behind as she crouched on the passenger seat.

They pulled over to clean up, grab coffee, and gas up at a rest stop north of Lake George. She used the last bit of cell connection for the next few hours to ring up a North Country source, a chatty Republican burgher she'd met years ago on a campaign, whose unrequited crush on her she'd managed to sustain at a distance for almost two decades.

When she asked him about the Plattsburgh property development, he emailed her an entire dossier in fifteen minutes. She downloaded it all at the rest stop and read it while they drove through the dark, piney void of the Adirondacks.

TDLC purchased the property of a defunct wallpaper mill in 2015, the same year they bought the legacy news brand. They had quickly restored derelict warehouses and nineteenth century brick ruins into a series of sleek, black, windowless warehouses. A high chain link fence surrounded the grounds, and the area was lit up all night so the compound's glow could be seen for miles, like an alien spaceship. The place hummed all day and night.

It was all pretty fucking weird, but the company had provided two hundred construction jobs and a significant number of security jobs to the hard-up families in the community.

It was no secret to the community that the place was a bitcoin mining farm, taking advantage of Plattsburgh's cheap renewable electricity from the Saranac River and the local tax exemption for religious enterprises.

For the past year, the money farm had been sucking up more electricity than the town had ever used. The previous winter, during an "Arctic Bomb" weather system that lasted almost a month, all the deviated wattage required the town to purchase electricity from another grid. Household electric bills spiked up 70 percent in one month. People were pissed but no leader had intervened.

Marjorie knew a lot about some things: the Iraq War, ISIS, who's who on the National Security Council, the names and numbers of various ambassadors, which strategists to call to find out what candidate was being paid off, and which one was having an affair and with whom, but what she knew about bitcoin would not fill a paragraph.

Lochinvar, though, he knew about crypto. He was crypto in every sense—cryptic, secretive, hidden—and fluent in the foreign language of algorithms in which the currency was based. And now she had him to herself for another 150 miles or so to the Canadian border. He had to help.

"Tell me about bitcoin," she said. "I know you understand it."

"Why?"

"I think we're headed to a Bitcoin mining farm, and I don't understand what it's all about."

"Huh," he grunted. He didn't say anything. She reached her hand out and stroked his cheek.

"It's complicated," he said. "It's a game for math nerds and geeks like me," he paused. "A pretty profitable game."

"How does it work though?"

"Well, the people who invented it, and nobody knows who they are, supposedly, are like libertarians who believe no nation or entity like a bank or a regulatory agency should have any business in who or what or how or why people spend their money. Cryptocurrency is hidden. It's dark web stuff, for now anyway, but very soon, I think they want to take it mainstream—hedge funds, investors, speculators. It's going to blow up."

"How does it work, though? Why does it use so much electricity?"

"Think of it like a computer lottery game. There's a number, and if you guess it, you win a million dollars, right? To mine bitcoin, millions of computers run through quadrillions of possible very long numbers racing to land on the one number that earns you some bitcoin."

"Like a game, like the lottery?"

"Of course, it's shady. Why do you think it's called crypto, honey?"

Whenever he called her honey, she clenched up a little. She knew that's what he and his last official girlfriend had called each other. *Honey, yech.* Plus, she could tell he was enjoying yanking her chain, giving just a little bit, always withholding the crucial bit of what he would have to "kill her" for if he told her.

"It is poised to take off. Some pretty reliable indicators predict this latest surge is not going to stop. And that means a whole lot of money for the miners. Digital gold, that's what it is."

"Probably why the shady company that owns *NewsMag* is into it."

"Yeah, so what will you do when you confirm this? Are you actually going to publish about it?"

"You don't call me Lois Lane for nothing. What else would I do?"

"I don't know—blackmail them, flee to Canada, buy a chalet at Whistler with the proceeds, ski every day? I'd even come with you for that."

Whenever he talked about a future together, insincere and fantastical as it seemed, she felt deep happiness. And so, in that state of mind, she leaned back and watched the dark forest whiz by.

19. A GHOST TOUR

Plattsburgh, New York, 1:00 a.m. Wednesday

They rolled into Plattsburgh as the hour flicked to 1:00—a number Marjorie took as a good omen. They rolled through the deserted streets of the North Country town. Houses and lawns were decorated for Halloween; sheet ghosts waved in the trees. Marjorie was reminded of how people in her hometown always put out corn shocks, skeletons, cobwebs, and carved pumpkins in late September. They left them there until Thanksgiving, when they switched to Christmas lights that stayed lit until Easter. Pagan harvest habits flourished in real America.

Pools of streetlight illuminated a half-shuttered Main Street. They passed the granite bulk of a county courthouse, surrounded by a lawn and ancient great spreading maples with leaves at their fall peak. The temperature up here was at least fifteen degrees cooler than in Manhattan. Crisp. Marjorie was glad that she'd worn her warm coat and scarf.

The TDLC complex was a few miles on the other side of town, down a long stretch of road through a flat that looked like stubbled corn farmland. They spotted the development from a great distance. Lit up, surrounded by a chain-link fence topped with razor wire, it glittered like a giant diamond or a prison.

"He didn't warn us about the razor wire," Marjorie said quietly.

They drove on without saying anything. Steve didn't slow down as they passed the main gate with its manned guardhouse.

"Wait, stop, what?" she said.

"You don't seriously expect to go inside at this hour, do you?

"Maybe not, but I didn't drive up here to wait until morning."

He gave her a curious look. Marjorie knew there was a part of him that she didn't access that followed the rules, that was, in fact, of the rules. Occasionally, he'd let slip how he thought of her as a marauder—too reckless, a bit disrespectful.

"Up ahead," she pointed to a shed and driveway. "You can do a turnaround there."

"These plates will be on camera if we drive up in there," he said. "And the rental car is in my company books."

"Okay, just drop me off at the edge of the road."

They drove back around, and he pulled over. He seemed
nervous and unsure. She stepped out, then leaned back in.
"Don't worry, honey. I won't give you away. Go get a coffee
and come back in half an hour."

He pulled away, and as the car receded she became aware
of a big noise, like the sound of a jet engine. It increased as
she walked into the circle of light. There was stirring in the
guardhouse, just one man. *Good.* She approached confidently,
black heels clicking on the asphalt, cashmere coat swinging,
Moroccan lamb wrapped around her neck, squared shoulders,
lipstick on, and eyes ahead.

She got to the door just as it opened. An older man in his
sixties, maybe, blinked warily, looking like he had just woken
up, which, of course, he had. He stared at her. She felt sorry
for him. Without TDLC and this humming electronic money
farm, he'd be a greeter at Walmart.

"Ma'am, what can I do for you? Did you run out of gas?"

"Hello! No, no. We did have a little traffic getting here, but
I'm with the TDLC headquarters in New York." She pulled
out a *NewsMag* card and flashed it at him.

He cast a farsighted eye at it. "This here says New Media Inc.
I'm sorry, ma'am, are you…"

"Yes, yes, TDLC is our parent company. You can look it up."

He peered again.

"Look, I know this is odd, and I can come back tomorrow
morning," she said. "But I've been sent up here to liaise with
community leaders. Say, do you happen to know Daniel

Stroutmeier?" The name of her supremely well-connected local Republican seemed worth dropping here.

"Of course, everyone knows Stroutmeier. He's good people. Why?"

"I was meant to give him a tour tomorrow. Oh, gosh, I cannot believe the thru-way traffic. A semi-trailer jack-knifed at Albany. Hellish delays. And now, here I am five hours late, and tomorrow morning, I will look like I don't know what I'm talking about."

"There's not much to see, ma'am, he said. She could tell he was relenting a little. He was scanning the bank of monitors above his little desk. She followed his eyes. Black and white images of aisles and aisles of machinery—not a human in sight. The jet engine roar of the system permeated the walls of the guard shack.

"I don't suppose you would," she gestured at the warehouses. "Just one? One peek. So, I don't look like too much of an idiot when I lead the politicos in tomorrow? We want them to like us." Persuasive word salad ran through her head: growth, economy, disruptors, more jobs, etc.

Harry, that was the name on his lapel pin. Harry looked her over again. She gave him her most winning smile and willed her face to glow with non-confrontational friendliness.

"Okay, then," he said, reaching for his flashlight and pushing out his hut's back door. "Wait." He went back to his desk and opened a drawer. "You'll want these, the cooling fans can blow out your eardrums."

She applied the earplugs, and followed him into a vast dim

warehouse. It was divided into long aisles of stacked blinking math machines. Hundreds, no, thousands of them. The roar of the cooling fans made human language nearly impossible. She snapped a few phone pictures as she walked behind him, enough to prove to anyone that she'd been inside a Bitcoin mine. They toured two aisles before he signaled toward the door.

Back in the guard kiosk, they removed their ear plugs.

"Wow, and twenty-four-seven," she said.

"That's right, ma'am," he said. "They never shut down. You know our motto: Money never sleeps."

"Hah! Yes, exactly, that is our motto!" she looked around. "There's not much to it, is there?" she continued.

"No, they just set the computers to on, and they're on their way to buried treasure."

"Mining away."

"Mining away," he agreed. "They say it's poised to take off in the market, but I don't know. I'm not burning up my paper money."

"You've been so kind," she said. "I think I've seen enough to look like I know what I'm doing tomorrow. Oh, and how many buildings are we talking about here?"

"Twelve so far, but I hear they're putting in another eight before the end of the year. Like I said, it's supposed to really take off this last quarter. But you know that."

"Yeah," she said. "Yes, I do. We sure got in at the right time."

20. THE FIELD OF GRIEF

Las Vegas, 9 p.m., Tuesday

Christopher Goodman stood alone at the edge of a vigil on
Sahara and Las Vegas Boulevard. Around him were flowers in
vases and strewn on the ground, bright mylar balloons, and
teddy bears. Hundreds of *santeria* candles in colored glasses
flickered in front of an altered True Grit Festival billboard
that leaned against the fence where so many had died or
been injured, a pair of cowboy boots with a halo painted over
each one. There were clusters of mourners and uniformed
police officers holding candles and handing out cards that
read #vegasstrong, their jaws clenched, blinking back tears.
No speeches, no sound except for the singsong of mass grief.
People consoled each other in group hugs. Adult men were on
their knees, sobbing. A cluster of mourners around a Harley
motorcycle club preacher in a black leather jacket worked
across the back with a cross of studs. He was reading from

the Book of Psalms in a sonorous tenor. "Merciful Lord, I am weak, but you are strong. I am burdened with grief; my heart is heavy; my spirit is crushed. Be my strength in times of weakness. Be my shelter from the storm."

Fifty yards away, as close to the Mandalay Bay sign as they could legally get, a large flock of men, women, and children from The True Word Church (based on their matching t-shirts) sang hymns. They seemed to be in a joyous trance, Goodman thought. If he didn't know better about the provoking circumstances, he'd say they were in a state of pitched ecstasy.

Was this what they meant by a state of grace, a process by which grief is transformed through some chemical-emotional alchemy into joy? Goodman knew all about how some wounds are not physical. His Catholic family had abandoned religion when he was a boy before he got confirmed. He had never felt the absence of religion as a deficit. But he had no idea how to find the solace these mourners sought.

A saying that an old editor had sometimes repeated came to him: "The job of a journalist is to comfort the afflicted and afflict the comfortable." Goodman could recall the man's face, his bulbous red nose, and tie and collar, which seemed to strangle the flesh under his chin. Dave Schultz had died of heart failure weeks after the newspaper where he'd spent forty years of his life folded.

Goodman could afflict the comfortable, but he had never been one to comfort the afflicted. He was constitutionally incapable of it because he felt too much. His Achilles heel and his secret superpower was that he was a sponge for other people's emotions. It terrified him and was a useless kind of empathy locked inside. People who knew him well had seen him cry. The rest of the world thought he was as sensitive as a brick wall.

He stepped into the keening crowd, weaving around the candles, teddies, and flowers. He was on his way to meet Alfred Sloan, another ex-military. Sloan was a JAG in Iraq, and when he left, he joined the SEC. As soon as his military pension kicked in, he quit the government. As he put it, the whole system had gone bad like a bottle of milk. It stunk to high heaven. Now, he was a vocal, active libertarian.

Sloan was very much a man who moved in Meadows's circles; if anything, he was more paranoid. He invested only in gold, collected weapons, and owned a Cessna. He owned a shooting range where he hosted the Aerospace Gun Club, which he had founded. Membership was by invitation only. His clubmates were early retiree white men who had worked for the big defense contractors. Lockheed, Boeing, Raytheon, nuclear weapons test cowboys who missed the days of above-ground testing. A few of the Space X kids came out to the desert range to shoot and drink with them, but mostly it was OGs.

Sloan had suggested meeting at the Skyfall Lounge at the top of the Delano, a shiny rectangular slab among the palms and pools on the 120-acre Mandalay Bay Resort grounds. Goodman crossed the resort without incident, again marveling at how quickly normalcy had been restored. He spotted Sloan at the bar. He was hard to miss with his head of thick white hair, deep tan, lean figure, and hatchet jaw. He was sipping a glass of something gold. No craft cocktails for him. He waved Goodman over and complained about the oversized hipster ice cube in his glass. What a way to water down a thirty-year Oban!

Goodman ordered a draft beer.

Sloan had last seen Meadows at the shooting range a month ago. He'd never been particularly social. Some of the guys took their wives on cruises or to the occasional gathering at places like the Skyfall. Meadows wasn't that kind of a couple's buddy. He tended to show up with very young, lithe women in thigh-high boots and dresses like shiny Christmas wrapping paper who made the wives uncomfortable. "More of a guys' guy," Sloan said. His jokes about whores made some of the born-agains squirm. Meadows was a much more devoted gambler than most of the men, who had retired to the area for the desert air, not the slots and roulette. He lived and breathed statistics. He bragged about how easy it had been to beat the machines.

"As far as I'm concerned, the guy was laundering money," Sloan said. "And as far as I'm concerned, it was nobody's business why or where it came from. The US government has no place in a man's wallet. But a piece of shit who slaughters people like that," Sloan's voice caught. "A man like that forfeits the right to be left alone."

Goodman nodded without speaking. He didn't feel much kinship with this man despite their shared experience in the military. Sloan belonged to the crowd—not small—that had abandoned all hope in the possibility of American institutional decency. He'd gone rogue in his own way, just not as feral as Meadows.

"Anyway," Sloan continued. "I'm sharing this with you because no one in the fake news ecosystem is reporting this guy right. I'm not saying I think you *will*, but I just think I ought to do my part. Those kids," Sloan choked up again and checked the emotion with another slug of Scotch.

He extracted a slender computer bag from a hook under the bar. "Anyway, I got you some stuff, more than seventy-five SARS here." He handed Goodman a printout of a spreadsheet of Suspicious Activities Reports that Meadows's banks had filed with the SEC.

"And here," he reached into a file and pulled out a sheaf of papers, "are his bank accounts. The SARs didn't result in anything. I guess the government paper pushers and keystone cops deemed it was all legal, if they even bothered to check."

Goodman laid the stack of papers on the bar and riffled them. From the first page, he would see that Meadows had dozens of bank accounts. As required by law, his various banks had repeatedly filed reports on suspicious five and six-figure deposits over ten years. None of the reports seemed to have resulted in any further investigation.

Sloan watched him and took a swallow of his dwindling drink. "I imagine when you get back to Washington, you'll be able to round up someone in the belly of the beast who will already have pulled all this for the FBI. But I'll bet you the whole MGM Grand that you'll never find the man or woman who will admit to signing off on the decision not to follow up. Mr. Meadows wasn't an Abu Anything. He wasn't an Ivan. He hadn't pissed off any Senators or crossed any of their donors. So, end of story—right there."

Goodman nodded. "Well, this is helpful. It's a good road map."

Sloan laughed.

"Road map to nowhere."

"Maybe. Maybe not." Goodman reached into his jacket and pulled out the picture of Bill Meadows in Guatemala with the team of CIA pilots in 1981. He slid it over to Sloan.

"Recognize any of these guys?"

Sloan peered at the picture and ran his finger along the captioned names. He looked surprised.

"Well, hell yeah, okay! So, he flew for Ollie North's Air Force back in the day. I'm not surprised. I might know some of the others." He peered more closely at the old black and white. "Yeah. There's Howard, too."

He looked up at Goodman. "Where'd you get this?"

Goodman didn't answer. Instead, he asked, "Who is Howard?"

"Howard Russell, with the agency in the seventies and eighties. He retired in New Mexico twenty years ago. He occasionally came to our club's golf weekends. Had some kind of slow cancer that speeded up in the end. Thought he wanted to be buried with his secrets, I guess. Not sure he's still kicking, actually."

"And the others?"

"Nope. Sorry. I don't recognize them." Sloan laid a twenty on the bar, stood up, and reached out a sinewy-tanned arm for a firm handshake.

"You know what I think? This guy is a hole straight down to hell. If you feel like digging that kind of hole and then climbing down inside it like Alice chasing the rabbit, be my guest! I've done my duty."

Sloan snapped a salute and walked off. He wove around L-shaped couches and sunken seating islands with an athletic gait Goodman envied. The bar was filled with shiny young people; magnums were sweating in ice buckets on pedestals, and oysters towered on platters. The old warning danced unbidden into his head: "Don't eat the fish if you can't see the ocean." Meaningless in the age of dry ice and jets, of course.

Goodman turned to the little sheaf of documents and peered at the small print. He'd seen these types of reports before. An attentive reader could learn a lot from them. Like court filings, with SEC documents, it paid to have keen near-distance eyesight and the ability to focus on every line—and the kind of memory that retained LLC names and their managers. Many relationships were hidden in plain sight.

He noted the names of the various banks where Meadows had accounts: sixteen accounts at Wells Fargo, ten at Chase, fifteen more at HSBC, a dozen more accounts in a variety of regional banks from California to Texas, and multiple trading accounts at Ameritrade.

He turned the page: investments. He scanned the list and, at first, thought there was a misprint. Line after line, Meadows had forked over millions to one company: TDLC. His portfolio was strangely lopsided. Suddenly, Goodman remembered what was nagging him—The Temple of True Divine Light Chiropraxis!

He almost heaved up his beer. *Steady. Steady, boy.* How could he have forgotten this? Denial, of course.

He pulled out his phone. Approaching midnight in Vegas, it was nearly 3:00 a.m. in New York. Would it do any good to wake Vera, the "love-muffin" young, tattooed managing editor, and discuss this with her? He didn't know how long it would take the swarm of national and Vegas ace reporters poking into Bill Meadows to come across the fact that the mass shooter with the highest kill count in American history was heavily invested in a holding company that also owned *NewsMag*. They couldn't be far behind. Would they care? Umm, yes. The same *NewsMag* that the FBI had raided one day after the shooting?

Connection?

How was it that he had never tried to figure out who or what owned the company that paid his salary? He had tacitly accepted the publicly known story that an obscure cult, like the Moonies, had put up the money to restart the legacy brand. Had he done due diligence? No.

It was a job, and they promised to let him do it without interference. The aggregation of American mass media meant only six companies produced 90 percent of it. How much worse could a cult be than the Murdochs, the Comcasts, CBS, and Disney?

Goodman looked at Vera's number for another beat, then hit call. Two rings, and he heard her voice, not as pert as the one at the morning meetings.

"Hello, Chris."

"Vera, sorry to wake you up."

"No problem. What's up?"

"I'm in Vegas but about to fly to Albuquerque."

He said it before he realized that was his plan.

"Thanks for letting me know," she replied sarcastically.

"Hey, better late than never. I've got some sources out here. I figured I had to come. I've learned a few things."

"What's up?" She sighed.

"I've got a lot of good leads, but I found something you need to know about right now."

"I'm listening."

"The guy worked for TDLC, you know, The Temple? And grab the smelling salts; he's been sending them his casino winnings."

"What? Sorry. What? The holding company for New Media Inc.? Our TDLC?"

"Is there another one?"

"That doesn't make sense."

"Nothing ever made *less* sense than a crazy cult paying our salaries, if you think about it."

"But you're saying the shooter paid *them*?"

"I don't know! The bank records indicate Bill Meadows transferred millions of dollars to TDLC over the last five years."

Vera let out a low whistle.

"Whistling women and crowing hens often come to no good ends," Goodman blurted. "Sorry, my dad used to say that to my sister."

"I think I'm already at a very bad end," she replied. "A mass shooter has paid our salaries?"

"Maybe. Banks suspected Meadows was money laundering, but the SEC never filed anything, at least not from the records I've seen. His TDLC investments make no sense unless he has some kind of ownership stake in the company from when he worked there."

"He worked there? Wait, wait, he was a member of The Temple?"

"No idea. He worked there for about five years until 2015 when they got into the media game and hired us."

"Screenshot and send the documents. I've got Marjorie DuBois on this story. I need to add this."

The name set Goodman onto a different astral plane: Marjorie, 3:00 in the morning, laughing in a sari of hotel sheets. A silky feeling washed over him, then evaporated.

"Oh, Marjorie, on a story about what?"

"I've assigned her to investigate the FBI raid on our offices."

Goodman couldn't help himself. He laughed out loud.

"Right now? That sounds suicidal, job-wise."

"Yeah, I guess she doesn't care. And neither do I, to tell you the truth. Anyway, good going, text me the pages now if you don't mind. We've got work to do. I want this online for the morning shows. And Chris, it's been nice working with you. I mean that. You're a pro. Thank you."

21. A LONG DEEP HOJO SLEEP

Plattsburgh, 3:00 a.m. Wednesday

Marjorie shook security guard Harry's hand, saying she hoped to see him tomorrow. Oh, but he worked the night shift. She walked beyond the circle of light and into the darkness at the edge of the road—utter stillness and chill. She pushed back against a feeling that Lochinvar had abandoned her. He was just that unpredictable. He'd seemed unusually shaky when he dropped her off.

It was very cold. She buttoned her coat to the chin and hugged the muffler tighter. There was no sign of him. She was about to text him when her phone lit up: Vera.

"Geez, you really do never sleep!"

"Marjorie?"

"You got me in the hyperborean zone."

"Huh? You made it up there? I cannot wait to hear what you find. Look, I'm sending you something, and I…"

"It's definitely a bitcoin mine. They're mining money. A very big mine."

"Crikey."

"Yeah. So, I've got a story, a small one anyway. We have enough between Eisen's trail of LLCs and this place. But are you up for that? I'm sure they won't like it."

"Hell, yes, but there's more. Goodman is in Vegas and…"

"Chris? Why?"

Marjorie had not exactly steered clear of Christopher Goodman since taking the job at the same company, but their interactions were infrequent. She never saw him. Once in a great while, she asked him for a contact, and he always obliged. If he harbored any hard feelings about the way she'd played him, he left them out of their virtual office. Lately, now that she was being played, she felt a little ashamed when she heard his name.

"He went cowboy on us. He flew out there without notice this morning. I guess he has some sources in Nevada. Anyway, he got enough for a fresh profile on the shooter. I doubt I will be around to edit it, but there's one bit you need to know. It's going to blow your mind."

"Do I have to wait for a text to know what you're talking

about?" Marjorie huffed steaming breath at her bare fingers.

"The shooter not only has worked for TDLC, he was also transferring his gambling money into the company."

"The Temple? What the fuck?"

As she spoke, headlights appeared around a curve in the road, and Lochinvar pulled up in front of her, rolling down the passenger window.

"How much for a blowjob?" he said, leaning over to open the door.

"What was that?" Vera said. "Did I hear someone say blowjob?"

"No! Uber driver! Snowjob."

"Hmm. Okay, well, I'll be waiting up. Can you file a story by 6:00 a.m.? I've just texted you Goodman's documents."

"You bet."

He leaned out the window.

"How'd it go, Lois Lane?"

"Great." She crawled in.

"Sorry I'm late. I got a little lost. I scoped out the lodging options and got us a room. Not the Quality Inn, I'm afraid, a HoJo."

He put one hand between her legs and steered the car into the black North Country night.

An hour later, Marjorie crouched at a tiny desk under a tiny lamp's circle of light, typing away on her laptop. A sated naked man dozed nearby. At one point, he sat up and reached a long arm out to caress her leg.

"God, I love sleeping to the sound of you writing," he said drowsily. "The click-click-click of your thoughts becoming words. It got into my dream. It turns me on."

When she thought about it later, she would decide she had never been happier than at that moment in that orange and blue room that reeked of stale cigarettes and where a bio-blacklight would probably reveal streaks of dried jizz on the walls. She had not before that instant understood her greatest desire: that this man she was in love with would love her back not only because he found her sexy in bed but also sexy in mind.

The sky was dark violet when she finished her piece and sent it to Vera. She headlined it: "FBI *NewsMag* raid mystery: #vegasmassacre connection?" The article incorporated Goodman's findings, which connected Bill Meadows to TDLC. It included the company's origins as a nineteenth century cult, its transformation into a tax-exempt corporate entity, and, apparently, bitcoin mining operation.

Her eyeballs burned. Her mouth tasted like the ash-flavored Keurig pod blend she'd sipped cold for the last hour. For the first time in a while, she craved a cigarette. She had none on her because she knew her lover loathed them. She went into the bathroom, stripped, and stood under the hot shower, letting the water boil her shoulders red. She brushed her teeth with her fingers and gulped water from the faucet, cold

Saranac River hydropower.

Looking in the mirror, she counted the new lines. She was getting old.

She thought about what she was giving up: her job, income, and probably the Manhattan apartment. Investigating the company was like a snake eating its tail, a fool's errand. It was always possible that some editor she'd once worked with would see it as heroic and haul her in from the cold. But the truth was, the idea that she might never again work didn't wreck her the way it would have even two years ago.

She left the mirror behind and crawled into bed. Lochinvar stirred. She felt the melt begin, another half hour of sleepy, sexy, reckless abandon, then almost darkness.

But he wouldn't let her sleep. He wanted to see the story she'd written. She groaned, reached up, and handed him the laptop.

"Have at it."

She watched him read.

"Say it," she said.

"Say what?"

"Admit that I'm the most interesting woman you know, that you will never, ever meet anyone as interesting to you."

"Why should I admit that?"

"Because it's true."

"It's true, but maybe I am for you, too."

She sighed. Her eyes were closed. It was never enough.

"Good as far as you got, but you didn't explain the *why*."

"Oh, God. The why of what?" She wanted to sleep, but now he was talking. She propped herself up on an elbow and watched his mouth move.

"Bitcoin. It's the future, you know—digital gold."

She yawned.

"This is important! Wake up, sleepyhead. You are witnessing the beginning of the end of centralized governments. In the West, we're dying of civilizational diabetes, too much of everything, fat, lazy. This is how we begin to exit the centralized government system and build something better that makes us individual and responsible again. Blockchain unlocks the digitization of *everything*. We're already at the point where all forms of communication—audio, video, letters—are reduced to electronic packets. Every bit of information, scarce assets, stock, bond, passports, and birth certificates can and will be blockchain-ified."

She watched him, intrigued. She'd never seen him quite so animated. It was like he was shedding a skin, and another animal lived underneath.

"And the best thing is to get in now, and it will be worth hundreds of trillions of dollars in a few decades. It is on a path to becoming the center of the world economy, like gold in the medieval economy."

He stopped and looked at her. Something in his expression was more assessing, less sheepish than usual, serious, almost triumphant.

For a moment, the room felt cold. The paranoia that afflicted her when he was out of sight: Who was he?

"Well, thanks for the Bitcoin lesson," she said, pulling the covers tighter and over her head. "Why did you wait until now to tell me you're invested? Are you mining it, too?"

"It's exciting! I like you, Lois Lane. That's why. This is progress, honey. There's nothing you or I can do about it. It's like standing in front of a train, holding out a hand, and yelling stop. Who does that besides Superman? Why would you do that when you can hop on the train and ride it to a better place?"

He carefully closed and placed her laptop on the bedside table. She leaned her head back on the pillow. *Honey*, how that word irritated her, but she forgot about it as he ran his hand up the side of her leg and whispered something filthy in her ear. His touch produced a rush of delicious relaxation unlike any before. She felt a tingling on her inner thigh. Then, a deep, dreamless sleep overtook her.

22. A TERMINATION

Lower Manhattan, 9:00 a.m. Wednesday

Lola Chatterjee's day started the night before. Busy as their busy professional lives were, Lola Chatterjee and William Roth maintained a fairly strict evening routine. They both made a point of returning to the West Village townhouse by 10:00 p.m. There, the Jean Georges Vongerichten-trained chef made a vegan dinner for Will, who refused to eat anything made outside his home. He brought what he didn't finish to the office the next day. Lola would often have consumed an earlier dinner of a hard-boiled egg and a smoothie, the only nutrition her stomach could digest anymore. After the meal, they took turns walking Abercrombie and Kent. Then, they went downstairs to their gym, decorated by a team from Milan as a miniature Roman bath with an entire fresco removed in the eighteenth century from Paestum, walls of Carrera marble, and great stone basins imported from a *Castello* purchased as an investment in

Umbria. On cool nights, they swam in the lap pool and shared a sauna, which was also Italian tiled, cerulean.

They had completed this routine and were in the master bedroom. Lola was on a yoga mat in the center of the vast white carpet, doing a set of physical therapy moves her doctor had suggested could help heal her stress-ravaged intestines. So far, the poo pills had no effect, but she was willing to give her gut biome five full weeks to be transformed as the specialist had suggested. They were discussing this hope when her phone went off.

Lola picked it up and stiffened. From her body language, Will could see it was someone from "upstairs" at her company. As she answered and listened to the caller, he watched his wife's olive skin turn several shades paler.

"What do you mean, someone we know is poking around in Plattsburgh? Who?"

She was quiet. Then, "I see. I see. Yes, of course. I'll handle it first thing."

Pause. Blink.

"Yes, by first thing, I mean now."

She tried, but Vera wouldn't answer her calls. Short of tracking the young woman down in Brooklyn, she had no options. She had no idea who was doing what in Plattsburgh. A few hours of wide-awake paralysis ended with the buzz of her phone against the Ceylon ebony of her bedside table. She had only just fallen asleep. It was so early it might as well have been the night before.

The pre-dawn buzzing didn't stop even after she opened the phone and started scrolling through the messages. She opened the most recent one first, which was from the CEO asking if she'd fired them yet. Before that, there was a public announcement from TDLC LLC denying any connection to Bill Meadows and a text informing everyone that the announcement was already in the inbox of every TV booker and editor on the planet.

She scrolled up through a thicket of texts from people whose names she only recognized from the corporate directory, discussing the draft statement. CIO, CEO, assistant vice president of finance, assistant vice president of communications, everyone had weighed in. How had she slept through this? She who never slept.

The phone was ringing now. They wanted to speak to her—needed her. She ignored it. She had to see the offending article. She scrolled up and finally found it. *Click.* An article by Marjorie DuBois and Christopher H. Goodman connecting TDLC to the Vegas shooter and a Bitcoin farm in upstate New York. She clicked over to the in-house click-tracker. By 7:00 a.m., the story had already been opened 500,000 times. Engagement was strong! The average length of time of eyes on the text was an astounding three minutes. It was not only the most-read story on the site, but it was also trending on Twitter.

A cramp unlike any she'd ever experienced sent her staggering to the toilet. Will stirred.

"You okay, babe?"

"No! Noooooo," her groans tapered off into silence, then flushing. Then, he heard the shower.

Vera was waiting in her office. She had been mildly surprised that her key card worked. The company managers must have been too busy with crisis management to block her.

She had published Marjorie's Plattsburgh report online with a co-byline by Christopher H. Goodman. She hadn't heard from either of the star reporters and wondered whether she should check in with them when Lola appeared at her door. Without bothering to knock, the content director strode in. She looked perfect: black hair shellacked into the tightest bun, another Anne Klein executive pantsuit, this one royal blue with the stiff cuffs and the collar of a white shirt peeking out, dressed for success with eyes like black ice. She stood a foot away from Vera's desk.

She snapped her fingers in place of a hello.

"I must ask you to retract and run a correction." She threw a sheaf of paper on the desk.

"And then please sign your termination document. Security will be in to escort you out in five minutes."

"Good morning!" Vera leaned back in her chair. "You're getting an unusually late start. You missed the morning meeting."

Lola glanced at her phone, which was vibrating nonstop, and backed up. "Four and a half minutes, now."

"Sad. Remember all those speeches about speaking truth to power and letting truth-tellers do the work? You even had me believing for a while."

Lola didn't flinch or change her position.

"No company would stand for this."

"Right, but by your metric of success, this is the most successful article we've ever published. Think of the advertisers before you take it down. We're approaching a million engagements and ten times that in social media shares."

"Don't make this difficult."

"Oh, I won't." Vera took her pass off, laid it on the desk, and shouldered her bike messenger bag.

"Wait!" Lola moved to block the door.

"I'm sorry, but security will have to search that bag before you leave."

Vera laughed out loud.

Beyond the glass wall, Vera could see the staff she'd led for these last few years. All eyes were on her office, watching. She caught Brickett's eye and winked. He gave her a sheepish wave and a thumbs up. She'd already said her goodbyes; this was one morning meeting most of the newsmaggots had not missed. They had crowded in, wall to wall, all phones buzzing with queries from friends, parents, and media reporters looking for tidbits. Vera calmly explained the situation: She'd assigned Marjorie DuBois to look into the raid. *NewsMag's* advertising revenue had financed a Bitcoin farm, and Goodman in Vegas had accidentally come across the link between the shooter and their parent company. Good teamwork!

None of it explained the FBI raid, of course.

That was as far as they'd gotten. Vera expected that was as far as they *would* get, at least on *NewsMag's* site. What did it mean? Who really were the owners? Other reporters might advance the story. It was leading on CNN (Vegas shooter connection) and Fox (liberal media associated with false flag operation?). *The Times* and *Wapo* had posted their own stories with links to the report.

"Maybe someone else will get to the bottom of it," Vera said. "We should all thank Marjorie and Chris for their courage."

"But they committed job suicide!" Brickett shouted. "And brought the whole damn *NewsMag* down with them! What about us?"

"What are we supposed to do?" one of the interns wailed. "What about our references?"

Vera had done what she could to reassure them. She was fond of her staff. The younger ones had learned a few things. It wasn't the end of the world. The older staff had managed to hang on for a few more years with health insurance.

No experience was ever wasted.

As she wrapped the meeting, some were crying. Glassy-eyed, others wandered out the door back to the newsroom, where they huddled in groups, weighing their options. Some loaded up their belongings and left the building immediately.

The great screens on the walls that ranked their stories by click and engagement were black for the first time in a few years.

In her office, with the staff watching, Vera thought of how it would play out if she pushed Lola out of her way. She had the benefit of weight; Lola had the benefit of height. An image of them tussling flashed through her head, and she laughed out loud.

"Looks like we got ourselves a Mexican standoff," Vera said. "I'm not signing anything," she pointed at the termination document. "And I'm not handing over my phone or laptop. They're not company property, but you can keep this."

She dumped the contents of the messenger bag on the desk. Loose OB tampons, coins, a pack of Advil, an opened half-pack of crackers with cheese, and a Twix fell out. A vape pen. And a lot of crumbs.

"There," she said. "Lucky for you and me both, I didn't bring my phone with me today. Have at it."

Vera could see the security guards approaching—the gloomy pair from downstairs, one stout and Black and one chalky and skeletal, a lifelong smoker on his last job. She felt sorry for them in their gray uniforms with the building's address embroidered across the right breast. They didn't know any more than she did who paid their salaries. She wondered if it ever occurred to them to ask.

"You could have stayed out of this," Lola said. "Just think about what you threw away. You and your newsmaggots, you could have played in the sandbox forever. You know? We asked so little of you."

"Looks like it's time for me to go," Vera said. She walked out to meet the guards.

23. ZERO VISIBILITY POSSIBLE

Plattsburgh, NY, 11:11 a.m. Wednesday

The Plattsburgh Hojo blackout drapes were very effective. Marjorie woke to a Stygian vacuum. She closed her eyes and opened them again. No difference. She closed them again and tried to retreat into studying the central conflict of her dream, the same strange dream she'd had all week: walking along the Hudson River in New York, except that the park was lush, almost tropical. She had been following a man, who was following a dog, and both dog and man were walking at the very edge of the dappled water. In the dream, it seemed imperative that she catch up to them and identify herself. She had the impression that the man was looking for her in the water. But no matter how fast she walked, they remained the same distance apart. She had been trying to speak, to shout and tell them, "I'm here. I am right behind you. I am not drowned." She woke herself up shouting, "Turn around! Turn around!" The man didn't turn.

She opened her eyes again. Black.

For a terribly long time, she couldn't remember where she was. She tried to orient herself from her position on the bed. If at home, the bathroom would be just down the hall to the left. But there ought to be a sliver of light under the door. She ran her hands along the edge of the bed. The smell of stale cigarettes brought her back to place.

Ahh, yes. He would be right over there. She felt across the bed, scuttling to the other side. No body. Nobody. She was, apparently, quite alone.

In the dark, she grabbed for the bedside table and finding it, crawled her fingers along to the base of a lamp until she felt a switch. She flicked it up. The room appeared. What time was it? There was no digital clock. She was sure that was not right. Where was the clock?

She heaved herself up. She felt strangely woozy, in fact, slightly nauseous. She lay very still and fought back the urge to retch. When she felt herself under control, she rolled her legs off the bed and stumbled over to the window. She took a handful of the thick black plastic and hauled it back. The midday sunlight was an affront; she had to close her eyes and lie back down. How had she slept so soundly? What happened to her internal body clock that buzzed at 7:00 a.m. no matter when she'd gone to bed? A surge of adrenaline coursed through her and went head-to-head with the wooziness. Now, she knew she was going to be sick. She staggered to the bathroom and heaved up a stream of brown water—cold coffee. After a few minutes on the floor, she recovered enough to stand and splash cold water on her face. She looked in the mirror to see her ashen face.

Back to the bed. Eyes closed. She felt around on the table for her phone—nothing. She eased her head up and scanned the table. No phone and, worse, no laptop.

And no Lochinvar. No shoes, no jacket. No man in the blue mid-century modern plastic chair. Her clothes were draped over the chair, her coat hanging from a peg by the bathroom door. Her boots were by the door—neatly. So, he'd tidied.

Other than the clothes, there was no sign of what she'd been up to just a few hours earlier. Or had it really been just a few hours? The sun was high, the sky crisp as a slap. The trees were vermilion and gold. Peak leaf-peeping in upstate New York.

She grabbed the phone and hit 0. One ring and a young woman's voice picked up.

"Front desk. This is Ashlee. May I help you?"

"Hello, ah, there doesn't seem to be a clock in this room. What time is it?"

"Oh, that's not right. I'm so sorry. Let me see. It's 11:11 exactly, ma'am."

Marjorie grunted. It was the only sound she could make. This should be a dream. *Jesus fucking Christ.*

She hung up and pushed herself to a sitting position again. She was naked. She looked at her thighs. A perfectly round brown bruise about the size of a dime caught her eye. She poked at it. No pain. *How strange,* she thought. *I don't recall slamming my leg into a tiny peg.* She poked at it again and realized it was a flesh-colored sticker. No, not a sticker, some kind of medical patch. She ripped it off. It left a bruise.

Other than that and the dissipating wooziness, she was in one piece. Except for just now, just now, the hole opened inside her, a terrible sinking of her stomach. Lochinvar had ghosted. He was gone, well and truly, with all her gear. A crazy desperation surged through her. She went wild, tearing sheets off the bed, shaking out the comforter, pounding out the pillows, and flipping the mattress, the chair cushions, and the closet. She crawled the carpet, running her hands over it to see if she felt the rectangle of her phone or the square of the laptop underneath.

Then, from the floor, across the room, eye level to her beside the foot of the desk, she saw her purse, right where she'd dropped it. *Oh, oh, thank you, surely.* She snatched it, and even as she lifted it, she knew that there was nothing heavy inside. She dumped it on the bed. Instead of her gear, two folded sheets of paper fell out, covered with Lochinvar's trademark tiny writing—the neat, ultra-legible all-caps of a man used to debugging code and filling out spreadsheets. There was something else—a small, thick packet. Her phone? She tore it open: a social security card with a woman's name on it, not hers; a driver's license with her picture on it, name and a DOB, not hers; a passport, also with her picture on it, same name, not hers; a bank card with the same name on it, not hers; and tacked to it, a four-digit code, presumably the pin. There was also a wad of cash, thousands, in hundreds.

She threw the pack at the wall and laid the unread handwritten pages on the desk. She popped a Keurig pod into the machine and hit brew. Then, she stood in the shower and let the icy Saranac watershed pour over her head and shoulders until her ears hurt.

Afterward, she rubbed herself raw with the thin Hojo towels and wrapped herself in the Hojo comforter. She poured the hot brew into last night's crusted Styrofoam container, took a few gulps, and finally felt ready to read.

Dearest Marjorie,

You've often said you wondered who I really am. I'm going to tell you as much as I can. Your suspicions were right; I am not just a computer scientist. I do know my way around algorithms. My job is to study networks. You know that I know everything about your network. I know who your sources are. You should know that we have all of them covered. You sussed that out. I knew you would. You're one of the smartest women I know. Maybe the smartest.

Marjorie almost threw her coffee at the wall. He was *still* playing her like a violin, even now. She read on.

You can go back to New York, but I'm not sure you will like what's waiting for you there.

One thing is that you don't have to worry about the videotape therapy sessions. I took care of all that. What were you thinking, letting them record it? But also, it breaks my heart that I made you hurt. You made me crazy, too.

A little about me, this is going with open source, so I'm not giving away classified information. My program is called Oculus. It's advanced AI. It sees everything and predicts behaviors, trends, prices, and even elections with the data we feed it.

Even with all this, this eyeball, centralized systems of control in the real world are breaking down—as they must. The West is dying. Many of the limbs—Congress, universities, civic life— are already gangrenous. Individuals and individual actors with great power are stepping in where it crumbles.

We are creating a new system where the defunct world of paper regulatory systems failed. We are on the cusp of a new, decentralized world. Centers of control will be cryptic and diffused. No one will see them. And I happen to work for one of those new nodes. And trust me on this: It's better for you if you step away. These are critical times. There are many doors in the mission. You step inside the wrong one, and you'll be lost. Trust me.

Why am I telling you all this? Because I am truly sorry that you're waking up alone. I wish I could stay and keep my arms around you. I would have liked to say goodbye. I left you with a future. There's a lot in the bank, enough to keep you comfortable, and we'll be refilling it. That key card has GPS coordinates to the dream house I mentioned up in Canada. Get a new start. Forget me not, honey. Keep an ear out for my knock on the door.

Gut punch. Down on the floor, hard to breathe. She closed her eyes and willed herself calm. Think. Think. You've been through worse. No, not really. Deja vu—hadn't she always known it would end like this: him gone and her, Marjorie DuBois, vaporized, just like that. A long time passed, until she focused on the blue and orange fibers of the carpet, inches from her eyes. On the floor. *Floored.* Fuck that. Rage and conviction replaced despair.

She dressed. After slugging back the rest of the cold and ghastly Keurig brew, she went down to the front desk. The woman who had answered her earlier time-check call lumbered out from a back office. She was maybe thirty-six, and nose-ringed, had pink and purple hair, and a shirt badge that read "Ashlee." Marjorie wondered whether this desk clerk had experience with hotel guests who'd been robbed of both a sense of time and phone and laptop. *Probably!*

She asked if there was a computer for guests. Ashlee directed her to the "business center," a closet-sized room near the gym and its tiny pool, reeking of chlorine. Once online, the first thing Marjorie discovered was she no longer had an email account at *NewsMag*. Then, she noticed her social media accounts—Twitter and Facebook—were also inaccessible. She had the same password for all of it, a bad habit that her cyber friends had warned would get her hacked. The password no longer worked.

She switched over to her personal email. That, at least, was still intact. So, they were leaving her with a choice—free will. She could reach out and call for help and rejoin the fray. She clicked on the inbox. And there it was, a series of emails from Vera: checking in, checking in, checking in, where are you? You okay? Then, she saw the subject line "SACKED," followed by a note saying she, Goodman, and Marjorie no longer had jobs. An email from Lola Chatterjee officially terminating her with a boilerplate from a company lawyer about the NDA. There were a few emails from some of the newsmaggots, high-fiving her on the story and congratulating her on the firing. Brickett, for example, had sent her a note saying how outraged he was that she had been fired by email and not in person. He was planning to look for another job immediately. So was half the staff, he said.

No email from Goodman. Well, he probably wouldn't, she thought. They weren't chums.

She went out to the front desk. She had an overwhelming need to make a to-do list and needed some paper. She also inquired about coffee in the area. The Keurig pod just wasn't going to do the trick. Ashlee pointed behind her at the glass door. "There's an Arby's and a McDonald's right out there across the highway and a Sheetz if you want to walk another quarter mile."

A fucking coffee desert. Marjorie looked out the revolving door. There was a distant highway with trucks shrieking past. She was suddenly famished.

"You missed breakfast," Ashlee said.

"I did. Slept in. Very comfortable bed!"

"Thanks for saying that, hon! Hey! We work at it. Wait here a sec."

Ashlee disappeared into the back office and returned with two granola bars and an apple wrapped in plastic.

"Here. Enjoy!"

Carrying the bounty back to her room, Marjorie choked back a little sob—the kindness of strangers.

Back at the tiny desk, she took up a pen. The same pen Lochinvar had used to write his letter to her, she thought with a pang and set it to paper. Her internal organizer, the machine that clicked on during deadlines in the field, had never failed her in an emergency. It tricked her into a sense of control. The to-do list went on for almost a page. She stopped twice to wolf down one and then the other granola bar.

Heavenly!

When she was finished, she leaned back, peeled the plastic off Ashlee's apple, and ate it, watching Fox with the sound down. The network broadcast had reverted to its local station. New York Capital Region Albany Fox was covering the story of the missing woman in New York City. The woman's NYDOT driver's license picture was on the screen along with a phone number to call if she was seen.

Marjorie squinted at the picture.

"Could be me," she heard herself say. "But not."

24. LUCKY ACRES

Albuquerque, 11:00 a.m. Wednesday

Chris Goodman was in an aisle seat, bouncing down over the desert. He left his hotel in the pre-dawn cool, the streets were void of life. Waiting for the taxi, he surveyed the crime scene. The little shrines of teddies and flowers had metastasized into a colorful day-after mountain of debris, a field of sorrow waiting for the sanitation trucks.

He had not known that Vera would byline him, and he might have liked to have had a choice. Would he have objected? Now, he had no one to publish his discoveries. He didn't know how he felt about the fact that he and the mass murderer were somehow connected.

He wondered about Marjorie. Where was she? Being fired with her gave him a certain hopeful buzz. Maybe they'd have something to reconnect over. He crushed the thought like a cigarette butt and turned to his immediate goal.

Autopilot. The only thing to do was keep flying. He couldn't consider the alternative—yet. He had located Howard Russell at an address in Albuquerque, not far from Kirtland Air Force Base, home to America's and possibly the planet's largest cache of nuclear weapons. There, one would find Howard Russell who, according to Sloan, was possibly dead but who knew Meadows "pretty well."

He had booked the first flight to Albuquerque. Half an hour after landing, just beyond a diner with an atomic mushroom as its logo, his Uber driver was turning off a four-lane highway into an unfinished subdivision. A sun-faded billboard at the entrance advertised:

LUCKY ACRES
Homes on two-acre lots, starting at $150k.
A fine place to raise a family and keep a horse.

Some wise ass had whited out the Y and turned the L into an F. No one had bothered to clean it up. Fuck Acres, a fine place for Howard Russell, retired CIA pilot, to come to die. Maybe.

The driver turned on a street of identical, seemingly vacant starter homes planted in grayish sand on which a few hardy high desert weeds had taken root. At the dead end of the street, the driver slowed.

"This is the number, but…"

Goodman checked his notes.

"Yup," he said. "We have arrived. Wait one minute."

The house didn't look occupied. But as Goodman approached, from the cement patio, he could see an open case of cans of Ensure on a kitchen table through a picture window.

Target locked, he thought. *Someone's in there.* He waved the Uber driver on and hit the doorbell. No sound. He rapped on the door. There was a long silence, the morning sun cooking his back, glinting off the picture window, distorting his reflection. He rapped again, harder. The silence was unnerving. It occurred to him that maybe Howard Russell had consumed his last Ensure a while ago.

He walked around to the back of the house and climbed a short staircase to a raised deck. There were more signs of life: a terra cotta planter base used as an ashtray, overflowing with stubbed out menthol Marlboros; more Ensure cartons, empty; an empty box of surgical bandages. As he was poking through a stack of what looked like medical bills scattered on a lawn chair, the back door suddenly flew open.

Goodman saw the gun first, instinctively flung himself down on the deck, and rolled off the edge to shelter under the edge.

"ID!" a raspy voice barked from the door. "Identify yourself."

"Sergeant Christopher Goodman, Army, Sir! Retired, sir!" And then, "Sloan, ahh, Sloan sent me."

"Sloan? That sneaky fuck."

There was a quiet beat. Then, Goodman could hear a squeaking, shuffling noise—rubber wheels on wood. He understood. Russell was rolling out the door in a wheelchair.

"Better *not* be US government, IRS, or the fucking county sheriff!"

"No, no, nothing like that." Goodman raised his empty hands above the edge of the deck.

"Well, come out from under there and show your face, man."

Goodman uncurled from his crouch and peered over the deck. Howard Russell, he assumed, wore his long gray hair in two braids and an untrimmed white beard going yellow at the ends dangled to his chest. He was emaciated, the color of dust, but with burning blue eyes. Skeletal albino blue legs with dirty bandages around both calves protruded underneath a khaki t-shirt and Hawaiian print trunks.

He held a Glock. Goodman assumed it was loaded.

The man's health was clearly under par, but something about the eyes told Goodman the guy could still move fast with that pistol.

Goodman eased his way back onto the deck. He didn't dare extend his hand but hoped he had arranged his face in the no-threat expression honed during his interrogator days. He tried to quickly take the measure of the man. It occurred to him to wonder if confronting a man with a Glock was worth knowing whatever he might find out, especially since he probably had nowhere to go with it. He put that thought out of his head.

"You are, I think, Howard Russell?" he started.

"I am," the man replied. He looked down at his bandaged legs and inched one bare foot with gnarled brown toenails off the wheelchair pedal momentarily. He winced and pulled it back. "I was, anyway."

"Look, I'm not here to do you any harm. I think you know that by now. Would you mind, you know," Goodman gestured at the gun. "It's a little hard to focus."

"Yep, so I wasn't expecting a visitor, and with what all's going on, you know, I got a right to protect my property—my home, my castle, my domain." Russell tucked the gun into an Indian beaded leather sack dangling from the wheelchair handle near his shoulder.

It was within a few seconds' reach, but Goodman relaxed slightly.

"Sloan didn't warn me to be ready for my closeup and a personal interview," Russell said. The accent was a little nasal, a little drawl, and maybe mid-Atlantic. Goodman tried to place it. Baltimore?

"No, but I needed more context after Sloan told me where you lived. And since you don't seem to have a phone…"

"Context—that's a big word."

"Well, just your piece of it," Goodman said. "That's all. Tell me about Meadows."

"Why would I know a Meadows?"

"I have a picture of you standing with him at an Air America landing strip in Honduras. Anyway, Sloan thought it was you." Goodman handed him a copy of the photo.

"Ah, that was a long time ago," Russell said. "And what makes you think an old man has a memory that long?"

"Look, I don't know if you have a TV here, but…"

"The massacre? Yeah. Okay. My opinion of Meadows? He was a bush pilot running drugs from Central America for the CIA. I heard he lost his pilot's license. I don't know why. I lost track of him for a decade or more."

Goodman kept still, waiting.

"My two cents: A *Sicario. Comprende?* They destroyed his records and some of mine, too. They know the truth. And so do I. That's why I keep this," he patted the beaded leather bag, "right close."

Goodman kept his hands in view as he leaned back on the porch rail and eased himself lower until he was seated. He was suddenly and immensely tired. The futility of the task flashed before him.

Who is this *they* of whom you speak?

Whatever Russell was going to tell him, it would never be enough, just another door out into the wilderness of mirrors: Sisyphean FOIA appeals year after year, the records released in dribs and drabs if at all but always redacted, the pro bono freedom of information lawyers growing older every year and on their deathbeds still raving about unprovable conspiracies. Years flipped like calendar pages in an old movie until he too was a written-off wackadoodle, an old man in dirty shorts with bandaged sore-flecked legs in a wheelchair, parked in some dusty Fuck Acres subdivision and, if he was lucky, with a gun in a beaded pouch hanging off his wheelchair handle.

The older man softened perceptibly as his adversary weakened. He kept his shrewd, suspicious eyes on Goodman and, without looking away, spoke.

"You look a little parched, son," he said. "Go on in and get yourself a drink if they haven't turned off the water yet."

"Yeah, I'm not used to the desert," Goodman said. "It's been a while." He looked down at the barren yard and the barren lots beyond it. There was not a blade of grass; not even a scrap of sage had taken root out here.

No man's land.

He went inside. The kitchen was surprisingly clean. He guessed the old man wasn't doing much cooking. He'd only need one glass for his Ensure. Goodman ran the tap, filled a cup, and drank. The water had a funny, metallic taste. Savor of failed desert subdivision.

He rejoined the man on the porch.

"Okay, so let's talk about Meadows."

"I told you I lost track of him a while ago."

"That's fine. Let's go back to a while ago. What can you tell me?"

"Well, that's up to how much dirt and shame you can stomach, I guess." The old man scratched gently at one of the bandages on his leg and was silent.

"I've got a pretty strong stomach."

"Ever smell a pile of human beings in a cage, half alive and half dead?"

"No. Did Meadows?"

"That, uh, was probably the least of it."

"Where?"

"Look, we were sent down there to move materiel, and we find, as usual, ourselves on the wrong side."

"Yes, like Vietnam, go on."

"We all, well, we all acclimated differently. It also depended on which of the colonels you were working with. Meadows had the one with the collection of human ears."

Goodman knew he was talking about El Salvador and Honduras before his time, but there were older guys in the DIA who had worked on training the men who became the death squads down there—total vileness, a shitshow.

"Have you ever met a sadist, Mr.… What did you say your name was?"

"Goodman. Chris Goodman."

"Goodman. Good man. Have you ever witnessed psychopathic sadism practiced on helpless men and women and stood by?"

"I have not."

"Didn't think so, but it does do something to you. They come back in your dreams. For me, well, only once, and I was out of there. I refused to fly back down to that fucker. Meadows, he went back quite a bit."

"Did he…" Goodman didn't know how to phrase it innocuously. "Did he like it?"

"I don't believe so. No. I guess maybe some people just pack it in tighter. I can tell you that standing by as a woman is taken out of a three-foot box, gang raped, and shoved back in—that does something to a man."

"So, what are you saying? Meadows had PTSD?"

"I don't call it that. It's not a medical condition, good man, don't let them tell you. It's a moral sickness—white man guilt and self-loathing—because, see, he could have stepped in, at possible great harm to himself, of course. And he did nothing."

"How do you know all this?'

"We talked about it. Ten years ago, maybe more, a bunch of us hooked up for an ayahuasca ceremony in the desert. We were trying to clean our minds, see. And he vomited it all up. I didn't see him after that; I don't believe."

"Who ran the operation? Did they know he was cracked?"

"I think that would have been Buzzy and Cookie, prep school nicknames, a drugs-for-weapons business if memory serves. I forget their last name now. They were from a prominent Philly banking family and diversified into various industries. One worked for the State Department. The other ran the family business, which included logistics. Both were with the Agency, quite an effective team."

Russell shifted in his wheelchair, rearranged his bandaged legs, and looked to be in pain.

"What difference does it make? I wouldn't bet Buzzy and Cookie would still be in the game. They'd be in their eighties now and probably forgot about Meadows long ago. Guys get into the Agency out of what they tell themselves is patriotism, but in the end, it's about the river of money. The ends justify the means. Then, they're in league with butchers who take pleasure in pulling the wings off human beings they've turned into flies."

"And Meadows?"

"Yeah, well, now everyone will want him to be part of some op in Vegas when he's just an old spook who went off the deep end. People want things to make sense. And when they don't, they can't stand it. There's gotta be a reason."

Russell leaned back and let out a weak laugh, the bleat of a goat, and started coughing. The coughing continued so long that Goodman thought it would turn into a death rattle. Instead, the old man recovered. After catching his breath, he went on.

"Well, you came to the right place after all," he said. "I had a side hobby for a while. It was kind of fun. I do know they were moving into the PSYOPs and the disinformation game. You know, *soft power.*" He sneered, then started his laugh-coughing again. When he recovered, he unlatched the brake and rolled back toward the open sliding door.

"Nature calls. Standby," Russell said as he struggled to get the wheels over the doorsill. "I'm trying to keep my diapers dry. Wait here."

The old man worked his way in reverse through the sliding door. The sun glinted off the glass. Goodman waited for a long time. Something, surely, would come of this.

He heard the screech of the wheelchair sidling back up to the edge of the glass door. It slid open. The old man's hand emerged, clutching something small and black. He flicked it out. A bit of black plastic, a tiny memory stick, bounced, skittered, and flipped to a stop at Goodman's feet.

"Have at it," the old man croaked. "See if it matters. It's not much good to me in here."

Goodman palmed the tiny drive.

"I'm going to lie down now," Russell said. "I've shared my piece. Godspeed, good man."

Goodman walked around to the front of the house. He was alone and seized with a sudden existential panic, holding this little plastic stick of hell-only-knew-what information in his hand. The sun was burning his eyeballs, and he felt the beginnings of a debilitating headache. In the twenty minutes he sat on the blazing deck waiting for an Uber to roll into Fuck Acres, he thought of begging the old man for more water.

But he didn't think he wanted to face him again—The Ghost of Goodman Future.

25. UNTETHERED

Lower Manhattan, 11:00 a.m. Wednesday

The ride down the elevator was awkward. Vera tried to make
the guards laugh, but they took seriously the possibility that
Vera—and any employee in the building, really—could go
in for a last act of revenge. They'd seen it before, a sudden
button push, a mad dash for the stairs, and back up to kick or
spit at their former employers' glass door. They'd never had
to call for backup, but that's only because they were vigilant,
alert to risk.

Out on the street, the October sky was a crystalline vacuum. A
9/11 sky, New Yorkers might still say. A flock of pigeons chose
the moment of her looking up to change perch, soaring off
the cornice of one of the older low brick structures and arcing
upward in mysterious unison, a synchronized gray whorl. The
swoosh of wings was audible even above the grumbling traffic.

The ancient Romans made momentous decisions on signs just like this—birds in upward flight.

A good augur for commencing battle, Vera thought.

The US Attorney's office for the Southern District of Manhattan was only a few blocks away. Vera strolled without hurrying. The little memory stick in the side pocket of her yoga pants made a small rectangular bulge. She had counted on not being padded down, although thinking back on the guards, she wondered if perhaps she had been too cavalier. Anyway, she was untethered now. She could do what she had to do, what she'd been waiting to do for a while.

Vera had more sources than friends, although more of the sources thought of themselves as friends than she did. The woman she was headed over to meet was one of the few who qualified as both. They'd been in classes together, pre-law, when Vera was considering law school. This one had gone on to do it, had succeeded spectacularly, and became an assistant district attorney in the public corruption department.

Vera had made an appointment early that morning before going into the office, but after posting the exposé. Now, she heard herself asking about the raid, explaining the financial connection between the shooter and the company, and sharing the stick with documents gathered from years of the company's files. She had never been able to suss out herself what New Media was up to, but in four years inside the beast, she had collected a lot of leads. Sometimes, it looked like money laundering and sometimes like a giant e-commerce scam. She had concluded that whatever it was, it required a subpoena, and even that might not work. It was one of those enterprises operated by what Ted Eisen called "sewer rats," a shrouded class of private, law-skirting tools for hire, sometimes but not always double agents or moonlighting spooks. They were necessary cogs in the wheels of corporations and states, providing services that powerful entities needed but couldn't afford to be seen obtaining or doing themselves.

And now, maybe, morphing into what it had always been intended to become, a node in a misinformation op.

Having dropped off her little hoard of leads, Vera took the six train uptown to her apartment, where her bags were packed and parked by the door. A first-class Emirates ticket to Athens was in a backpack pocket with her passport. Her first stop was Lesvos and Sappho's town, a stone cottage she'd slept in once and always remembered, then purchased at a distance, now hers. Maybe in a month or a year from now, she'd travel to Exarchia, the cop-free zone where refugees, squatters, and anarchic plotters mingled. Maybe. There were so many places in which one could disappear and still work.

26. THEY NEED A SUPERHERO

Washington, DC, White House, Early Cocktail Hour, Wednesday

Preston Silver had to admit it. His life had turned around in the space of just forty-eight hours. He had charmed the *Washington Monthly* "40 Under 40" professor. He couldn't believe it, but she had let him kiss her and feel up under her skirt as they said goodbye on the corner of Wisconsin and M. Blissed out and giggling, she'd been. They'd closed down the Four Seasons bar. He'd woke up to a text—a suggestive peach emoji. There was no other way to take that; it was not subtle in the least. His groin twitched for the second time in twelve hours. After how long?

Executive editor was the cherry on top.

Now, back inside the West Wing, not too far from the Oval

(the Big Guy was not around), Silver was with someone far more important. He was being entertained, toasted, by the real brains of the operation.

Harrison Benson's White House man-cave was like the man, disheveled, a sanctuary of disrespect for norms. He had not deigned to move his library of revolutionary texts and medieval history in here. There were no family pictures of former wives and their mutual spawn. He didn't plan to remain in the belly of this beast for long. Just long enough, in fact, to do his best to blow it up from the inside. The shelves were bare except for a few empty forty-year Glenfiddich Scotch bottles that, when full, retailed for more than $5,000 each. A man-size cardboard Pepe the Frog leered from one corner. There was also a crookedly taped poster of the 1988 Super Bowl champion Redskins team. On it, someone had scrawled in black marker, "Fuck yeah! That's Redskins, Big Chief. I come in peace to RAPE your SQUAW!" It was difficult to make out the autograph. Three burner phones lay on the desk amidst piles of briefing papers and cigar stubs.

He was pouring several fingers of Scotch into a pair of Styrofoam cups. A dying ember of a stogie dangled from his smirking lips. Another cigar sent up a thin stream of smoke from Silver's paw. The return of smoking inside the White House was a thumb in the collective eye of decades of federal agency nannies.

Cuba Libre!

"Raising a cup to you!" Benson tapped his Styrofoam cup against Silver's and downed it in one gulp, frat-boy style. "Executive editor." He refilled it.

"Thank you, kindly, good sir," Silver replied.

He took a sip, savoring the pricey liquid, and swallowed what he reckoned to be about $100 worth. "I wouldn't have thought it tasted as good in Styrofoam, but it works."

"It's White House Styrofoam," Benson replied. "Special petroleum blend."

The two men contemplated each other in silence. Silver was wary. He was sitting with a Goebbels. If his kid was still talking to him, he might have had a hard time explaining this camaraderie, but he wouldn't have to.

And truly, one could make a case that it would all work out just fine for future generations.

Benson read his mind.

"It's weird, right?" Benson said. "I mean, two years ago, you wouldn't give me the time of day, remember?"

Silver kept his face impassive. He wasn't going to grovel.

"Remember? CPAC. We were all freaks to you guys then."

"I wouldn't go that far," the journalist replied. "Just… irrelevant."

Benson's face twisted for a millisecond then rearranged itself affably. The dark years of irrelevance were behind him now, but he could still *feel* the humiliation. He didn't like that feeling one bit. Revenge was best served cold.

He poured himself another Scotch and, this time, took a sip. He let the silence thicken. Silver coughed. Benson could tell he was unsure of his next move, even with his new title.

Silly new title, he might have added, but he didn't.

"I might have been irrelevant, as you noticed. In fact, I buy that I, as an individual, still am irrelevant in the widest sweep of history," he took a sip of Scotch, revving up his tone of sarcastic grandiosity. His face changed, and Silver saw the flabby old-surfer-boy baby face transmogrified into something feral. The journalist sucked in his breath and hid his shock behind the white Styrofoam cup. Then, it was gone.

"But here's what's *not* irrelevant," Benson continued. "There is a new game in town with new rules. You're a historian. You know that epochs begin and end and civilizations rise and fall. You probably wrote theses at Princeton about such points in history. You never expected to have a front-row seat on that sort of change. Yet, you now find yourself in that position. Just as I, irrelevant Harrison Benson, find myself in the position of doing a small part to make—no, not make—midwife, if I may use that douche-ey term, the change because it's coming.

"It's been coming on since the so-called Enlightenment when we humans decided to replace and then play God. For a few centuries, we managed to pretend the human race could thrive in a rational, science-worshipping world. But science doesn't have all the answers—and it never will. Humans are not rational animals; facts alone don't suffice. On the contrary, in the end, they offer nothing but despair.

"They, we, need a new superhero and new villain. The old legends are dead, no more cherry tree to chop down, no more he never told a lie. We need Marvel comics video game-style heroes and simple evil antagonists."

Silver could see Benson both did and did not believe in his analysis of history and the human condition. The game was that it didn't matter what was true and what wasn't. It was enough to sow doubt and distrust and present a strong boss-man into the mix with the answers. It took a minute to spew bullshit and hours, days, weeks to disprove it.

In this game, anything was possible, and anything could be true. Even a lie. Especially a lie.

Silver could see the genius of it. The American public was fertile ground, having been lied to over and over about everything from Cold War assassinations to whether Saddam had WMD. Maybe it had always been like this.

Benson was still waxing on, frat boy supercilious twang. "This is the beginning of the end of the centralized state. You didn't want the gold standard? Okay, then, no more government money for you, suckers! Which reminds me of the beauty of Bitcoin: Every man, woman, and child in America will have their own currency, their own birth certificate, and every legal document stored on the blockchain. No more lawyers, no more government."

"Err, okay," Silver smirked.

Benson sat back, re-lit his cigar, and checked his watch.

"Oops, I almost forgot. The boss is making a speech."

He shoved papers around on his desk, knocking a few to the floor, feeling around for the remote. The screen on the wall flickered.

The President was on Fox, calling in. "People are saying…"

and he was off with the word salad of the day. Bill Meadows had been photographed in a pink pussy hat. He supported crooked Hillary. He had canvassed for the Democrats in New Mexico. He was a socialist. Maybe Antifa? *Coming for your guns.*

The Fox News fake *kaffeeklatsch* in the fake living room nodded—bobblehead dolls.

Silver felt dizzy. Benson was right. It was all story. He'd known that reality was malleable. Hadn't he himself molded it in words like clay?

But this?

He stood up and shook Benson's hand like a good sportsman on the losing team. Holding the dead stogie in his other hand, he retreated to find a quiet place from which to write about the mass murderer, the Antifa in the pink pussy hat, and the deep state plant.

27. THE MANAGEMENT OF SAVAGERY

Albuquerque, 3:00 p.m. Wednesday

Goodman lay back on the hotel bed and waited for a handful of Vitamin I, Ibuprofen, to kick through to his bloodstream. He'd shut the blinds, but a strip of bleaching sunlight still oozed around the edges and found his optic nerve. He felt a strange sensation of intense urgency and a fatalistic pressure to do nothing. He'd known this feeling before in another country's desert light when sick and depleted, seething with the knowledge of a very specific evil underway that he was helpless to stop. He had not moved from a DIA trailer's rack for two days except to piss out the door.

His mind knitted and tore apart the threads of what he knew and didn't understand. The stick was still attached to his laptop, the screen blinking with lines of numbers he couldn't read, the foreign language of computer code.

He scrolled forward. Just page after page of code. Goodman scrolled until his eyes burned. *Fucking waste of time!* There were two things Goodman knew for sure.

One was that he was alone in a room with a story.

And two was that he didn't have anyone to tell it to.

Lola Chatterjee had released a statement accusing him of making up the connection between *NewsMag's* parent company and the Vegas shooter. Until he turned it off, his phone was vibrating with texts from curious reporters.

He had the document and the record of the financial connection between Meadows and TDLC. That would be easy enough to slip to another reporter, but where did that leave him? He was sure to be sued over the NDA, and he needed money. No reporters committee for a free press could save his ass; he was pretty certain of that.

It was too easy for Lola to accuse him of fake news and trafficking in conspiracy theories. Half the nation already thought journalists made it all up. The line between fact and fake had been scribbled out. He didn't even understand the connection between Bill Meadows, a mass murderer, and the corporate and/or intelligence op child of The Temple of the Emissaries of The True Divine Light Chiropraxis, TDLC Corp.

Then, there was the other angle. He thought of Marjorie, poking around in the bitcoin farm. What did any of this have to do with Bitcoin mining? Cryptocurrency was suddenly gaining in value, shooting upwards. The trend had been sharply up for weeks. Someone was making a fortune.

Was that part of the puzzle or just another unconnected random fact in the blizzard of events?

He was not immune to the lure of a unified theory.

Faith in linked random tragedies and a shadowy power center— CIA, Soros, deep state, KGB, FSB, Mossad, Black Cube—stood in for belief in God. But he clung to skepticism, demanding documents, proof, and evidence.

Why had the FBI raided the *NewsMag* office on the day after the deadliest mass shooting in US history? *It had to be connected, had to be, had to be—or not?*

Goodman let this ball of cat hair roll around in his brain until he felt the eight hundred milligrams of Ibuprofen melt the shards of glass behind his eyeballs. As the agony subsided into a manageable ache, he opened his eyes, sat up, and gulped a bottle of water.

Then, he grabbed his laptop and started scrolling.

On the worldwide web, he saw himself trashed publicly by the *NewsMag* content director. An online swarm amplified her allegation of his mental instability. Some were upping the ante, accusing him of being an unpatriotic trasher of the military going back to his whistleblower days. His personal inbox was filling up with emails from people claiming to be Iraq War veterans excoriating him. He had no way of knowing if any of them were real.

All of it was utterly predictable except for one element: Preston Silver.

Goodman hadn't been keeping up with Preston lately.
He'd apparently missed a full conversion. Before the 2017
inauguration, they had occasionally met in DuPont Circle.
Silver was rarely motivated to wander more than a few
blocks from home. They would convene for drinks, martinis
for Silver and beers and a shot for Goodman, and trash
their employer. They tore into Vera, made fun of Lola, and
laughed bitterly at the downward spiral of their profession, the
country, democracy, and the planet, generally, before toddling
off to their lonely lives.

However, Silver recently had gone full hermit. Goodman
hardly ever heard him snorting derisively on the morning
conference calls.

Now, suddenly, he saw that his former colleague had never
abandoned ambition.

Goodman's eyes popped as he read the unfiltered, uncorrected
commentary from Folkus and Benson—from the White House!
Meadows was a Democrat. Meadows was a deep-state plant.
Meadows had been photographed at the women's march in
a pussy hat and was, therefore, a Hillary supporter. Black
helicopters had been seen around Vegas with transponders off.

Additionally, ever so wee and low was a dog whistle. *Some
folks were saying* the Vegas massacre had been the biggest
gathering yet of crisis actors, probably cast and hired by
George Soros. It couldn't be proven, but then again, it
couldn't be disproven—not at this point in time.

Silver was flooding the zone with administration red herrings.
NewsMag had transformed overnight into a node in the lockstep messaging of the "counter-revolutionary" intelligentsia,
and Silver was the author!

The *pièce de résistance* was a statement co-signed by Silver,
now identified as executive editor and *NewsMag's* content
director.

Silver and Chatterjee—the dream team.

"Anatomy of an Op" was the headline. The publication
condemned individuals who would try to twist tragedies like
the Vegas massacre for political ends. They congratulated
NewsMag's parent company, New Media Incorporated, for
supporting real journalism. The publication would uphold
its legacy and maintain the strictest and highest standards of
truth-telling. There was no mention of TDLC.

Goodman picked up his phone and banged his thumb
into Silver's contact. One ring, two, three, then straight to
voicemail. He heard himself screaming.

"What the fuck? What the fuck? What the fuck are you doing?"

He threw the phone across the room and stumbled over to
the minibar. The eight hundred milligrams of Ibuprofen had
done the trick on his headache, but he needed more. He felt
the twinge in his lower back as he reached down and grabbed
a handful of miniature bottles, pulling out two gin and two
whiskeys. He poured the whiskey straight into his mouth,
downing it in two gulps. He put the gin on the desk for later.

No, now.

He lay back on the bed and closed his eyes.

It's happened, he thought. *Today is the last day of truth—or
maybe yesterday.*

28. ALBUQUERQUE SUNSET

Albuquerque, 6:00 p.m. Wednesday

Goodman came to consciousness at sunset, waking from a strange dream that involved an aerial view of chanting surging masses of people. One of those black and white reels from 1930s Germany, but somehow now. He didn't know where he was. He had to wait for memory and recognition to seep back in and to orient himself in the direction of the bathroom and the bedside light.

Then he remembered Albuquerque, the high desert. He pulled himself up, staggered to the bathroom, threw water on his face, then wandered to the window and pushed back the blackout drape. The neon of a diner sign, a grinning green chili with a thumb up. Lacework of of street light ending at the edge of black miles of barren, red New Mexico. Horizon, violet.

His dream of angry crowds vibrated behind his eyes. He felt
a surge of sorrow. The violet strip faded to black. The great
emptiness of the landscape was inside him. This was land they
all loved. How was it not enough just to be alive here and now?

He went back into the little drive. This time, with his
headache cleared, he could carefully turn each page, his habit:
slow, one at a time, patient. Code, code, code, code, code
for a hundred or more pages. Then, finally, text. *Eureka!* A
PowerPoint presentation.

The cover image was stamped "GOVERNMENT
PROPERTY" and "TOP SECRET."

Of course, he expected no less from the Wizard of Fuck Acres.

The first page identified the creator:

> Terrell Communications Inc. was awarded an $850
> million Defense Threat Reduction Agency (DTRA)
> contract to support training, exercise planning, mission
> rehearsal, threat assessment and countermeasures, to
> bolster national and international security within the
> DTRA Nuclear Enterprise Directorate.

The next page was the presentation opener: The words
"WEAPONIZED NEUROSCIENCE" were superimposed
in day-glo lime across a backdrop of a black and white atomic
mushroom cloud.

Beneath that, it said:

> We have developed an arsenal of informational weapons.
> Before 2008, we had never tested them at scale. We have
> now found that human adaptive mechanisms can scale

catastrophically.

Well, that must have woken up a sleepy conference room somewhere, Goodman thought. He clicked forward: Magritte's faceless man in a bowler hat and a quote. "We use the same techniques as Aristotle and Hitler. We appeal to people on an emotional level to get them to agree on a functional level." –Oliver Terrell.

The next slide contained a pictogram titled "THE 3 As" with notes below:

> The tools of neuro-weaponry are the three As—ACCESS, ASSESS, AND AFFECT. In six decades of work on thought control, the mode of access to human brains relied on proximity—sticking things inside or aiming things at the human skull. This is no longer necessary. New research into cognitive processes offers ways to achieve the three As at a distance.

The next slide was an image of a smartphone and a man with wires coming out of his head.

> The fundamental enabler of this change is the worldwide web, which serves as connective tissue through which effects are propagated. This digital substrate allows ACCESS to the human brain at a distance.

Next was a slide titled "THE BIG FIVE," followed by four bullets:

- Openness to experience includes aspects such as intellectual curiosity and creative imagination
- Conscientiousness includes organization, productiveness, and responsibility

- Extroversion (sociability, assertiveness) and its opposite Introversion (compassion, respectfulness, trust in others)
- Neuroticism includes tendencies toward anxiety and depression

The next screen was "Number Five," and contained a cartoon of a man holding his nose beside a cockroach on a pile of garbage:

DISGUST: Pique the sanctity/purity emotional state. Disgust is a powerful motivator for racism and other ethno-social reactions to outgroups.

The next slides were captioned "TERRELL LAWSUIT."

Exhibit 22, Blackwell v. Terrell.

Witness: The United States was an ideal petri dish to apply an analog biological metaphor for our experiment. The nation's loose data laws gave us access to the financial lives of hundreds of millions of adults, thanks to Axiom, Experian, Magellan, and others. Unregulated commercial data harvesting coupled with social media platforms gave us access to behavioral data that aided in the sorting process.

Exhibit 24

Witness: We figured out how to create online communities, segmenting people into what they called "fireplaces," groups as small as twenty-five people, geographically separate, linked by common psychographic profiles and social media influence levels. In this way, we created lie machines. Lies implanted in democratic discourse by authoritarians are often intended to be caught. Their primary goal is not to successfully deceive but rather to undermine the democratic value of testimony.

The next slide had "REAL WORLD TEST RUNS" superimposed over a photo of a riot.

In Haiti and Guyana, we found that mass disinformation campaigns can be augmented by events and catastrophes. Anything that inflames the amygdala, anything that increases panic and anxiety, makes certain recipients more receptive.

The final slide was company PR and a copyright claim.

Oliver Terrell spun his company out of a behavioral sciences laboratory he ran at Oxford in the 1990s. After 9/11, Terrell Communications marketed the company as a provider of strategic communications for a dangerous world. Terrell has won defense contracts from the UN, South Africa, Ghana, Kenya, Guyana, and Hungary and did behavioral surveys for the US military in Iran and Yemen.

The last line was the kicker: "In 2016, Terrell Communications was acquired by TDLC (NYSE: TDLC)."

Goodman sat back and laughed. How had no one picked up on the fact that the company that bought the shell of *NewsMag* in 2015 had next acquired a company specializing in weaponized information?

After the PowerPoint, there were a few blank pages, followed by a research paper titled "9/11, Orlando, Boston Marathon: The direct and moderating effects of mass murder anxiety on political and policy attitudes."

It included keywords: "emotions, anxiety, public opinion, guns, shooting, and terrorism," followed by an abstract.

> The researchers concluded that the anxious became *more* attracted to threatening information after news about a mass trauma. That conclusion was replicated again and again after news of mass murder.

> Tragedies prompt the surveillance system. For example, those anxious after the 9/11 attacks watched more television than the less anxious. In addition, anxiety about it produced greater interest in and attention to presidential campaigns.

Goodman sat back. None of this was really surprising. What theory was it supposed to favor, though? Was it surprising that somewhere in the government, someone had written a contract to study how mass violence worked with mass influence and political manipulation? No. They studied how to make viruses more lethal; they would study anything.

Did it suggest that a deep state was malevolently applying this knowledge in the real world to control?

He refused to go there.

Goodman lit a Merit. He skipped through the PowerPoint again. Neither the presenter nor the location of the event were named.

Goodman lay on the bed, clicked on the TV, flicked through the cable shows, and heard the breathless chirp of frightened animals. Their hyperawareness of the ticking clock before the next ad break was infectious. They radiated anxiety even when laughing at each other's jokes. This wallpaper of panic was inside every bar, restaurant, gym, kitchen, living room, and waiting area in America. Colored screens with their endless loops—if it bleeds, it leads—pulling in eyeballs: tsunamis engulfing cities, forest fires glowing apocalyptically, people jumping from burning towers.

It was mesmerizing.

Goodman had often thought about the effect of TV news death imagery on repeat. The ancient Greeks annually trekked with Persephone into the underworld and returned, with the aim of physical and psychic revitalization. Did moderns need that revitalization hourly?

Vegas, like 9/11 and Orlando and Boston and the practically weekly mass shootings, all served as ritual trips to the underworld. Hundreds of smartphone recordings were uploaded and viewed millions of times. The anxious grew addicted, returning again and again and again to be reborn through it.

Not me. Not me. Not yet. Not this time.

What did it mean that the company that had paid his salary also owned a company that performed psychographic experiments and that a mass murderer had been investing gambling winnings into it?

Goodman stopped himself at the very edge of conjuring links to make it make sense. *Nope, nope, nope. Don't go down there.* Randomness existed. It was the backdrop of human existence.

Unless proven otherwise, he would believe Meadows was just another human aperture into chaos—a lone nut. Of course, the lone nuts were the best assassins, and there was a long list of them. Some, like Oswald, were silenced before they could be examined. Picking a nutcase to carry out a killing, especially one who was also a sharpshooter, was a tactic "old as the Sicilian hills," a member of the New York Mafia once said.

Or the homeless woman who took a bus from Seattle to New York and shot the president of a failing CIA-connected bank while in some kind of trance. Her mind was so blasted— MKUltra? Schizophrenia?—that she didn't even know how she got to the East Coast or found her way up the elevator to the banker's office.

Meadows, though, was a lone nut whose mind and motives were now eternally untraceable. A man, like so many, who cracked and spewed death before vaporizing into the black hole. Impenetrable darkness. Searching for the explanation was a fool's errand.

Zero visibility possible.

He thought about his work as an investigator. Goodman had held fast to the conviction that chipping away at the edge of the unknown was always worth it. If the answer never came to him, someone else would come along and build on the known. And it was true, wasn't it, that exposing the corrupt and murderous means by which yachts, gated mansions, and offshore trusts had been acquired—that all still mattered?

But now, he thought half the nation—maybe more, polls didn't work anymore—believed his kind just made it all up.

In human history, it had never been easier to flood the zone with shit. Leaders had been trying to manage the savage for millenia, to little effect.

The Bensons of the world didn't deserve credit; they just had hubris and luck with timing. If they could buy a Silver and *NewsMag*, all they had to do was publish one or two *people are saying* stories occasionally.

It didn't take much—like a drop of ink in a glass of water.

29. HOUSEKEEPING

Albuquerque, 7:00 p.m. Wednesday

There was a knock at the door, gentle, then a little harder.

"Housekeeping!"

"Later, please!"

He looked at the clock: it was well past late checkout time. He didn't feel like moving on just yet. But now the phone by the bed was ringing.

"Mr. Goodman?" A front desk clerk asked.

"That's me, yeah. Yeah, I know. I'm staying over; just run the card for another night, please."

"Yes, sir, one moment please," a ticking of typing, silence, more ticking.

"I'm sorry, sir, but your card doesn't seem to be working."

"Ahh shit," he said. "Try this one." He pulled out another card and read off another number.

More ticking, and then, "I'm so sorry, sir. That card is also declined."

"God-damnit! Let me read it to you again."

The clerk got the same result. "I'm really sorry, sir. You should perhaps contact the company."

Of course, he thought, as he emptied the contents of his wallet on the bed.

Of course, this was how it was going to happen.

Of course, they couldn't shut down his bank account or his cards. Could they?

He thought about Snowden in Moscow—fucking pipsqueak traitor. Yet, he'd had an escape plan.

Think. Think, man. He felt himself reverting to training.

Dissociate. Focus. Strategize.

He closed his eyes, breathed in, and felt the familiar wave of cold logic replace the panic. *Breathe, box breathe, easy does it, there.* There was always an option until your heart stopped beating.

He opened his laptop, opened a file, sent it to his phone, and screenshot the numbers for backup. This was the red list, the "I gotta guy" list—the fixers and linkers. The network was sub rosa, and he'd not called on it before, although he had helped organize it.

There was another knock on the door and the same female voice.

"Housekeeping."

"Ahh, thanks, just showering, and then I'm out," he shouted.

Another knock. This time, it was a male voice, the first layer of muscle.

"Housekeeping! Mr. Goodman, we have to prepare for the next guest."

Goodman methodically dried off, folded his things, and packed the laptop. Uber didn't work; he'd have to make the contacts from down in the lobby. *Okay, okay,* he thought.

The stick was in his pocket and his electronics juiced. The line between fact and fiction was fuzzy, but he had a clarifying lens. There was one destination possible, a way station on the road to full rogue, just for a day or two.

Fuck Acres, here I come.

30. TAKE THE 11:11

Plattsburgh, NY, 11:11 p.m. Wednesday

Marjorie spent the day lolling in bed at the Plattsburgh Hojo. The pillows were as advertised: *dreamy*. She wasn't being lazy. She was good to herself in an emergency. She had long experience being her own stern nurse. She confined her goals for the day to nourishment, contemplation, and rest for the journey ahead.

She watched TV with the sound down. There was an update from New York City: the flashing lights of an ambulance parked beside the Hudson River and a body on a gurney under a white sheet. In the upper right corner was a photo of the missing woman: green-eyed, dark-haired, possibly found dead, possible suicide, forensic tests still underway.

It could be me, Marjorie thought.

She slept all afternoon and dreamed of walking in a gallery of black and white photographs. She'd forgotten so many of their names, but she recognized them. Ghosts materialized from the black screen of her laptop, where all their stories were stowed. The longing to tell her own was excruciating.

She came to as the late afternoon sun angled across the parking lot outside, varnishing the autumn trees blood red and gold. She was famished. She called down to the front desk for food advice. "Door Dash is your best bet," was the answer. The clerk recommended Fuddruckers down the street as the best and fastest. Soon, she was eating the best bacon cheeseburger, fries, and milkshake of her life.

The Adirondack from Penn Station to Montreal, making all scheduled stops, was already rolling north of Albany. It would pick up passengers in Plattsburgh at 11:11 p.m.—11:11—one-half of the binaries, ones and zeroes. The zeroes were the ephemeral power, invisible, the thin place. Now, "Marjorie DuBois" was just a set of letters, an online presence.

The mystery that she couldn't solve, that her mind was approaching and avoiding, was why he would want to erase her. It was true that she was tanking her career on her own. Did he think she was a loose cannon and would expose him? But to try to help her completely obliterate herself. She wracked her brain for some clue, something they had discussed, some piece of information that he'd let slip. Nothing.

She thought about Kara. They had been so close to the end. Of course, there was no "cure," only "management." Kara had taught her to think of her relationship with Lochinvar as an addiction, like heroin, the same physical obsession, the same possession by pleasure, and the same sickness of the soul. If she failed to show up, would the young therapist assume she had finally overdosed on love?

She imagined her lover cueing up the therapy video, watching her sob, rage, brag, and tell stories. She had, she realized, at some level expected he could hack it—almost hoped he would. She pictured him leaning back in his Eames chair, taking in her most personal, private thoughts and confessions of insecurity. Maybe smirking, maybe not. Another time, another woman would have been humiliated and furious. Marjorie realized she wasn't angry. She hadn't understood until now how desperately she'd wanted—needed—someone, no, not just someone, not just Kara, him, to *know* her.

We are all anonymous except for split seconds in a lifetime to our lovers, the ones who look for our faces in a crowd, and those who see us when we are not there. She remembered the sensation of her mouth forming a deep, helpless smile when he surprised her that time in Washington when she looked up from a coffee, and he was standing in front of her. She hadn't told him where she was, but he'd found her. Stalked she'd been, but happy. She might never see him again.

She showered, luxuriating in the hot steam for half an hour. She ran her hands over her body. Still, after all this, she was capable of arousal at the thought of him.

No, she was not dead at all.

She had nothing to pack besides the packet he had left her and a Hojo's toiletry kit. The taxi from the motel to the train station passed the same dark, old houses she'd only just traveled by with a lover and a story inside her, almost written. Now, she was someone with almost every story told—except her own.

She made her way up the station stairs and into a small pool of light on the platform. As the northbound train arrived in a windstorm, she took one last peek at the letter. The line about meeting again punched her in the heart with hope. She dropped the note into a trash can as the train doors slid open. A conductor swung out and lowered a stepstool.

"All aboard!" he shouted. "M'lady," he said, holding out his hand with exaggerated courtliness to the sole passenger.

She reached up, gripped his black-gloved hand, and boarded—without baggage. She felt clean and scraped. Winter was on the wind. There would be more of that farther on, soon enough.

This is the road sign that
inspired the title. Shot by
the author on a New Mexico
highway at dawn.